MISCELLANY FARRAGO

STORIES

AARON MORRISON

THREE ⫶ OWLS
PUBLISHING

ISBN 978-1-7331920-9-5

www.threeowlspublishing.com

For my fellow Storytellers

For those still struggling

For those still dreaming and creating

CHRISTMAS WITH JERRY

Jerry arranged the decorations just so. A cherished mix of family ornaments, nicknacks, and adornments he had collected over the years. Snowglobes and tin soldiers on the mantel. Garland and a nutcracker on the end table. A motorized Santa, who had long lost his naughty or nice list, in the corner. Jerry's eyes lit up and a child-like smile appeared on his face as he switched on the toy train and it began its cycle around the Christmas tree. Dozens of other ornaments, decorations, and trinkets looked on as Jerry all but skipped to his keyboards. He preferred an actual organ, but that was too impractical. Jerry had worked the dual keyboard setup just as well. The extra control over the sound, as well as the portability, had appealed to Jerry. Though it had meant purchasing stands, foot pedals, cables, amps, and the like, he had never regretted the decision.

Jerry sat on the folding piano bench and adjusted his large, thick rimmed glasses. A man in his 50s, he still had a bit of a youthful appearance about him. He attributed his boyish looks to the "magic and love of Christmas." He was roughly six foot three and relatively athletic. His hairstyle and outfit had more of a conservative Liberace look about them. Jerry had admired Liberace's showmanship, though he never went as colorful and extravagant. Jerry's black, crushed velvet suit and slightly frilly white shirt were about as wild as he ever got. He had grown up watching all those old Christmas specials, and various performances from his mother's era, and had taken inspiration from Jerry Lewis, Bing Crosby, and the like. He had wanted to learn to play the organ at the age of six, and his mother had obliged. Jerry was a natural, and took to the instrument quickly. Over the years, he developed his own take on the performance styles of his idols. Sure, there wasn't much money in what he did, but it brought him joy, and Jerry figured that was enough.

Jerry had finished adjusting knobs and settings on his keyboards, positioned himself comfortably, and began to play. "Rudolph the Red-Nosed Reindeer" flowed from the amplifier as Jerry's expert fingers danced over the keys. He swayed and danced in his seat, smiling. He added his own flourishes to the song liberally, preferring the jazzy, almost improvised, feel to music. He always liked to start off with something upbeat and fun, and this was a solid go-to. He pictured Rudolph, and Donner, and Dasher, and all the rest, frolicking in the snow to his music. His grin had grown even wider at the thought. He played through the song, finishing with a flourish, and a happy, satisfied little shake of his upper body and head.

Jerry made a few adjustments on his keyboard, readied himself, and started into his rendition of "Frosty the Snowman." Fun little offbeat riffs and pauses for the drum machine. Jerry swayed excitedly until, about halfway through the song, he got distracted, causing his usually sure fingers to miss, making an off key noise. Frustrated, he slammed his hand down on the keys, which caused an unpleasant squawk to emit from the amplifier. Jerry stopped the drum machine and looked over at what had distracted him.

In the corner of the room, the woman had started struggling again and had let out an unintended whimper. Her husband was still out cold from the injection of Midazolam Jerry had given him. The two children had been easy to subdue. The family of four lay there, arms bound behind their backs, legs tied at the ankles, and gags in their mouths.

Jerry, quickly and aggressively, strode over to the woman and knelt down, his face mere inches away from hers.

"Stop. Please stop." Jerry's voice shook in anger and frustration.

The woman's breathing had become more panicked.

"Just stop and enjoy the music!" Pleading had turned to demanding. "I'm just trying to spread some goddamn Christmas cheer!" Jerry removed a syringe from the case and brought it toward the woman.

She shook her head, eyes wide.

"Are you going to settle down and enjoy the music?"

The woman nodded. Tears continued to drip down her face.

"Good." Jerry put the syringe away. "Santa will be here soon, and we need to be in the Christmas spirit!" His voice had switched back to his usual calm and happy sounding tone. Jerry patted the woman on the shoulder, tousled the hair of her son, and skipped back to the keyboards.

He started back where he left off with "Frosty the Snowman," all the while smiling for his audience. He played a few more upbeat tunes, before eventually moving into the slower, religious Christmas songs. His somber approach to the slow songs was in stark contrast to the showy style of the upbeat ones. This went on for close to an hour, though Jerry did not concern himself with time. At one point, Jerry had gone back over to the woman, removed her gag, and asked her if she and the kids wanted to sing.

"Please let us go," she pleaded. Her voice exhausted and terrified. "We won't say anything. Please. No. No!"

Jerry replaced the gag and sighed. He looked at the woman with disappointment and sadness on his face. Jerry paused for a moment and returned to the music.

Eventually, after "Sleigh Ride," Jerry looked up and around at the ceiling excitedly, a smile on his face.

"Do you hear that? I think he's almost here!" He smiled and winked at his audience. "Here Comes Santa Claus" erupted from the amp, sounding as giddy and excited as Jerry was. He played through the entirety of the song and continued to play as he pressed a few buttons on the keyboard, and adjusted a few things on another device. The music looped as Jerry stood and clasped his hands together in exuberance. He smiled and left the room. The tune continued to repeat over and over. Jerry reentered the room, a Santa Claus costume over his black, crushed velvet suit, and a fake white beard over his face. Santa took a moment to appreciate the decorations and music before turning his attention to the family. With a sigh, he stepped toward them. The mechanical Santa moved its empty arms and watched on.

***

*inspired by RLM and BOTW

RESORT

Thomas Griffin approached the bus with some trepidation. He didn't quite know what he was getting himself into, but when Everett Langston offers you $100,000 to simply share your opinions, you don't pass it up. It was good money. All Thomas had to do was spend a single weekend with two other "experts" observing and critiquing Langston's new "groundbreaking project." In their initial communications, Langston assured Thomas that he and the others would find his new project to be astounding, especially given their individual areas of expertise.

Thomas thought it was a joke at first. He didn't feel as though he had adequate work experience, expertise, or knowledge to consult on an Everett Langston endeavour. Thomas hoped the chunk of change wasn't offered as a means to secure positive reviews from himself and the other experts. However, Thomas had built a reputation on his frank and honest opinions, and he was determined to share them openly and freely.

Thomas adjusted his bag on his shoulders and continued to walk toward the bus. Another man hopped out of the side door of the bus and gave a brief wave.

He approached Thomas.

"You must be one of Langston's other chosen few." The man extended his hand. "Maxwell Zader."

Thomas shook Maxwell's hand. "Thomas Griffin."

Maxwell looked like an everyone's-favorite-professor-type.

"Griffin... Griffin..." Maxwell seemed to be searching his memory. He snapped his fingers several times as something clicked. "Griffin! You're the uh, uh, uh, ghost guy! That's right."

"I mean, I prefer paranormal expert, but yeah." Thomas laughed slightly to make sure Maxwell knew he wasn't really offended.

Maxwell laughed as well. "Apologies."

"What, uh, field are you in?" Thomas asked.

"Counseling psychology, primarily. Doesn't quite roll off the tongue though."

"Oh. You're *Doctor* Maxwell Zader. You wrote the book, uh, *Grief and The Every-man*, right?"

"I did! You've read it?"

"No."

"Oh." Maxwell's excitement dipped to disappointment. His mood elevated again as he quickly tapped Thomas's shoulder with the side of his hand and pointed. "Looks like the third in our little crew has arrived."

Thomas looked down at his shoulder where Maxwell had tapped, surprised by Maxwell's immediate familiarity, then turned to look. Thomas's heart sank. He was instantly frustrated with himself for his reaction, but, in his defense, he hadn't exactly been prepared.

Maxwell moved just past Thomas to introduce himself to the newcomer.

Thomas took a deep breath, steadied himself, and turned around.

"Maxwell Zader."

"Stacey Carmichael."

"It's a pleasure." Maxwell gave a little bow with his head.

Stacey laughed, amused by the attempted charm. She turned to Thomas. "Griff." She smiled kindly.

"Stace," Thomas answered, surprising himself with how even he was able to keep his voice.

"You look good," she said.

"Eh. Trick of the beard." Thomas shrugged.

"Well, it's a good choice." Stacey nodded in approval.

Thomas noticed Maxwell's eyes darting backing and forth between Thomas and Stacey. A knowing smile appeared on Maxwell's face. He took a small step back and seemed to move into observation mode.

"Any clue what *exactly* we were brought here to observe?" Thomas asked.

"No idea." Stacey shook her head. "But if the two of us are here, it's gotta be something interesting."

"What do you do?" Maxwell inserted himself back into the conversation.

"I'm a parapsychologist slash... ghost hunter— I think that's the best way to describe it?" Stacey bobbled her head slightly back and forth as she answered.

"So we have two ghost people," Maxwell pointed at Stacey and Thomas, "and a grief counselor," he pointed at himself with his thumb, "hired by an eccentric billionaire to give our professional opinions on some mystery project." He pursed his lips in thought. "What could go wrong?"

The trio boarded the bus, and the driver started off once they had settled in. It was an incredibly fancy luxury tour bus, with plenty of space for the three to spread out and relax for the duration of the three hour drive.

Thomas had thought it excessive that they had been forced to meet up so far away from wherever it was they were going, but obviously Langston wanted to keep this project of his a secret. Whatever it was, at least Langston had picked a beautiful countryside setting.

Thomas watched the scenery blur by from his seat toward the back of the bus. He could hear Stacey and Maxwell's generic small talk before he put his earbuds in. His eyes drifted from the passing landscape to Stacey. She happened to look back at him moments after he had looked at her.

Stacey, though still clearly listening to Maxwell, smiled at Thomas.

Thomas smiled, somewhat sheepishly, back.

Stacey returned her focus to her conversation with Maxwell.

Thomas slowly looked back out onto the sweeping horizon and soon fell asleep.

Thomas was brought out of his nap when Stacey gently shook his shoulder.

"Hey. We're almost there." She nodded toward the front of the bus.

Thomas nodded in acknowledgment and rubbed the remaining sleep from his eyes. He pushed himself out of his seat and followed Stacey to the front of the bus.

Maxwell, already at the front, looked back and nodded at Thomas and Stacey as they approached. "Well, I suppose it's time we get to see what this is all about."

A giant temporary construction wall arched out from the natural tree line, hiding whatever was behind it. The bus came to a stop and waited for the gate to open. Once clear to move again, the bus moved forward, causing the trio to lurch forward slightly. The bus passed through the gate, and the trio leaned instinctively to get as good a view as they could. What they saw astonished them. They looked at each other in confusion.

They drove over a parking lot still under construction. Several new, beautifully constructed buildings stood in the distance. One, further back to the right, appeared to be a hotel. *Visitor Center* was written across the front of the central building. It was difficult to tell what the rest were from their current distance. A large arching sign read *Ultima Gradus*. Underneath those words, and much smaller, read *Resort*.

"The hell is this?" Thomas muttered in disbelief.

"Definitely," Stacey slowly emphasized each syllable, "not what I was expecting."

"Yeah, I'm uh," Maxwell continued the train of thought, in the same low volume as the others, "confused."

The bus pulled up as close to the main entrance as possible before coming to a stop. The side door opened with a hydraulic hiss.

"Well. We're here," said the driver. "Hope the trip wasn't too bad."

The trio retrieved their things, and one by one thanked the driver as they got off the bus.

Two figures approached, in discussion with each other, when the older of the two turned his attention to the group, smiled and raised his hand in greeting.

Everett Langston had a friendly grandpa look about him. "Welcome! Welcome! I'm so glad you all accepted the invitation!" He shook hands with all three of the group. "I'm sure you have plenty of questions, so let's get right to it, shall we? Alice, my assistant," Langston gestured to the woman beside him, "will make sure your bags get to your rooms. And, I would ask that you keep your cell phones away. Don't want information to leak too early."

Thomas and the others nodded in understanding.

"Well then!" Langston smiled excitedly. "Follow me!"

Thomas, Stacey, and Maxwell all shared a *here we go* look and started off behind Langston. They passed through the visitor's center, and the large ring-shaped desk labeled "check in." The building was fully constructed, but not yet filled with any brochures or literature. They exited through the back and entered into the main area of the resort. Langston pointed out the shops and dining areas on the right. The hotel and "relaxation and meditation" areas at the back. Everything was sleek and modern, yet somehow seemed to fit in well with the natural forest and hills surrounding the resort. While clearly a lot of money was put into the place, Thomas noted that nothing seemed gaudy or outrageous.

"So, as you can see," Langston continued his tour, "we wanted to build a state of the art facility, while still bringing in the natural beauty of the land. It's really the perfect location, well, for several reasons. Ah! Here we are."

They had walked to the left side of the resort and circled around behind an area that was still under construction.

From what Thomas could see, it appeared to be a garden-like area, with plants, fountains, walkways, benches, and such. Not all the landscaping was done, but it looked beautiful nonetheless. The garden was enclosed by a dome made of clear pentagonal panels. At the edges of each panel, a thin amount of some silvery metal filled the seems. Thomas thought the metal appeared to flow slowly in all directions, and he swore there was a faint hum coming from the structure.

They arrived at the back of a building at the far edge of the resort, many yards away from the dome. Langston put in a code, swiped a key card, and, after the distinct sound of unlocking, ushered the trio through the now-open door. They walked down a hallway, and entered what appeared to be a control and observation room.

The room was fairly large, accommodating the now seven people comfortably. A mounted desk ran along the entire length of one of the walls. Several monitors and a soundboard sat on top of the desk. Neatly bound wires and cords ran from those devices to computer towers below. Above the desk, a window had been installed, which also reached from end to end and up the rest of the way to the ceiling.

A man and woman, who Thomas assumed to be technicians, checked various settings displayed on the monitors. They adjusted levels on a soundboard-- generally made sure everything was running properly.

Another man stood in the room, supervising the technicians.

Langston, who kept his voice down so as to not disturb the proceedings, informed the trio that the man supervising was Steven DiAngelo.

"He's the one that helped make the magic happen, if you will." Langston whispered.

Thomas observed the two technicians and DiAngelo. Thomas felt his job was to look for deception. He always assumed everything was a trick, whether intentional or not, until the possibility could be ruled out.

The techs just seemed to be doing their job, but DiAngelo put off an uneasy energy. While Thomas couldn't determine if it was deception without interviewing him, there was something about DiAngelo that Thomas didn't quite like. Where Langston was the jovial grandfather type, DiAngelo was the guy in the neighborhood that everyone was pretty sure had a body or two buried in the basement.

Granted, initial looks and impressions could be wrong, but Thomas operated from a starting position of distrust, for better or worse.

In the adjacent room, clearly visible through the window, was a smaller version of the dome that Thomas had seen outside. Inside the dome were two simple chairs, one of which was occupied by a young woman. She had a few sensors attached to her, which Thomas assumed were sending the vital signs Thomas saw on one of the monitors. Multiple cameras were pointed into the dome, showing the proceedings on another monitor.

Langston walked over to the male tech, who handed over a file folder. After returning to the trio, Langston gave them the file folder to look over. It was labeled AMANDA W. and contained some basic information about her. There were two photographs inside. One was of the young woman, Amanda, who was in the other room. The other was of an older man.

"Are you ready, Amanda?" The female tech pressed a button, and spoke into a microphone.

Amanda nodded her head.

"Ready when you are," her voice came through speakers in the control room.

The tech looked back at everyone in the room, specifically waiting for Langston and DiAngelo to give the go ahead. Everyone nodded their approval, and the tech turned back to the microphone. "You can start."

Langston waved the trio forward, and they all stepped closer to the observation window. The room was wide enough that they could stand at the desk.

Amanda took a deep breath, closed her eyes briefly, and opened them after she exhaled. "Grandpa? Are you there?" She waited a moment. "Grandpa Harold? It's me, Amanda. If you can, please speak to me."

Silence.

Thomas shifted uncomfortably.

Another moment passed of nothing. But then...

Thomas squinted and leaned forward. His hands rested on the desk. Something appeared in the chair across from Amanda.

It was a faint light blue light that gradually grew stronger as it took the form of a person. Features slowly began to appear on the figure. Thomas glanced back down at the file and the picture of Amanda's grandfather. The manifesting figure matched the one in the photograph, though it was translucent and glowed light blue.

Amanda gasped and covered her mouth in shock. She reached out with a shaky hand before quickly bringing it back. "Grandpa?" Her voice cracked, and tears had formed in her eyes.

The figure smiled and slowly nodded.

"I... I just wanted to say goodbye. I'm sorry I wasn't there. I'm glad you're here now though."

"It's good to see you. I am proud of you." If a voice could sound translucent, this was the example.

"Goodbye." Amanda covered her mouth again. She still seemed to be in shock as she began to cry, what appeared to be, happy tears.

The image faded away.

Langston looked at the trio excitedly. "Well? Incredible, yes?"

"It was, uh, certainly something." Thomas tried not to sound too skeptical.

"Definitely interesting." Stacey was always better at hiding it than Thomas.

Maxwell simply scratched his chin, unsure of what to say.

"Come!" Langston gestured toward the door. "I'll show you the device and introduce you to Amanda."

The trio followed the female tech out of the room and into the adjacent one. Langston followed behind.

Amanda was still seated, her hands cupped over her nose and mouth. She rocked slightly, smiles occasionally appeared at the edges of her mouth, clearly processing her experience. She looked up as the tech opened the door to the dome. Amanda stood up to exit, wiping away a few tears as she did.

The tech began removing the various sensors as Langston introduced everyone. "Amanda, this is Stacey Carmichael, Thomas Griffin, and Dr. Maxwell Zader." They each raised their hand in a wave in turn.

"Sorry I'm such a mess!" Amanda laughed, wiping away a few remaining tears.

"Don't worry about that," Maxwell said. "That must have been an incredibly emotional experience."

"It was." Amanda nodded.

"Were you and your grandfather close?" Stacey asked.

Amanda nodded. "Very. Made it extra hard not being there when he…" Her voice broke. She kept back her tears with a sad smile. "Sorry."

"I know you all must have more questions," Langston began, "but Michelle does need to run a checkup on Amanda, and well…" Langston's eyes danced in sympathy for Amanda's current emotional state, and a small, sad smile of his own flickered across Langston's lips.

"Could we interview you tomorrow, then?" Thomas asked. He partly wanted to continue questioning, but he had confidence that if her story was rehearsed, he could fish it out tomorrow just as well. "Assuming it's ok with you and everyone else."

"It would be fine by me." Amanda nodded.

"I'll have Alice set everything up for tomorrow then," Langston said. "And I'm sure you will have a list of things you will want to do tomorrow, which we can arrange later as well."

Once the schedule for the next day was settled, Amanda and Michelle left the room.

"So?" Langston gestured and looked impressed at the dome, "What do you think?"

"What's the trick?" Thomas let the skeptic out. "Advanced hologram projection, or something along those lines?"

Langston chuckled. "I read that you always take the doubter's approach. That's exactly why I wanted you here. But no. There's no trick. No holograms or projections."

"How does it work then?" Stacey inquired.

"So," Langston clasped his hands together, excited to describe his toy, "and I'm over simplifying things, the dome functions essentially as an EMF amplifier."

"EMF?" Maxwell shook his head.

"Electromagnetic field." Langston replied. "I'm sure our two experts," he gestured toward Stacey and Thomas, "would do a better job of explaining its connection to the paranormal world, but it is a naturally occuring wave of energy that comes from the sun, and from man made sources, like power lines, computers, and such."

"Is that safe?" Maxwell raised an eyebrow.

"You use a cellphone, right?" Thomas asked.

Maxwell nodded.

"You get a blast of EMF right to the brain every time you put that thing up to your head." Thomas tapped his temple.

Maxwell grimaced.

"As to your safety concerns, that's why, at least in part, we don't allow repeated uses of the dome." Langston rejoined the conversation. "There's some disagreement about the impact of prolonged exposure to EMF, but, and I know this may sound cold, we do have everyone sign waivers, just in case."

"So what does the EMF have to do with calling up spirits?" Maxwell looked at Thomas and Stacey for answers.

"Well," Stacey took the lead, "in paranormal research, a strong link has been found between high readings of EMF and paranormal activity. Usually when there's a cold spot, something falls off a shelf, you get touched, or whatever, there is almost always a spike in EMF readings surrounding the area. The theory is that paranormal entities use that energy to perform those various tasks." She shrugged. "High EMF doesn't mean ghosts are present, but usually when there is paranormal activity, there is high EMF. If that makes sense."

Maxwell nodded. "So, if you increase the energy source, you make it easier for them to do... whatever."

"Exactly," Stacey confirmed. "That's the theory anyway."

"What's this made out of?" Thomas had walked up to the dome, his face a few inches from the glass.

"Ah, yes," Langston responded. "Michelle could tell you more about the exact specifications, but the panels are made of a mixture of quartz, other crystals, and fiberglass. The metal seams you see are a mix of various alloys based on both alchemy and modern science. As power moves through the seams, it powers the panels. The panels send and reflect the EMF we were discussing which creates a vortex, if you will, that allows for the spirits to come through. As Miss Carmichael said, the energy then makes it easier for the spirits to manifest."

"So, it's like a modern, 3D, what do you call it, seance? Ouija board?" Maxwell queried.

"Well, this is science based," Langston smiled, "unlike those two things. But, if you mean a general sense of a means to contact the deceased, then yes. I suppose that would be correct." Langston looked proudly at the dome. "The thought behind the project was if energy is neither created nor destroyed, then there must be a way to harness that energy after a person passes on. Call it a soul, base consciousness, or whatever you want. This is giving us a way to contact that energy."

"So what's your interest in all this? Why build this entire place?" Thomas asked.

Langston nodded his head. "As you may or may not know, I lost my daughter and son-in-law in a car crash years ago. I, obviously, never got to say my goodbyes. This is for people like me. Like my grandchildren. Like Amanda. Like so many others that never got that chance. My hope is that this place will give people the opportunity to say goodbye and take those final steps in processing their grief and loss." Langston paused for a second. Sadness had crept into his disposition, but then he resumed his cheerful energy. "But we can discuss this more over dinner and make sure you have access to everything you need for tomorrow. Alice can show you to your rooms at the hotel. We can meet in the lobby in about an hour and then head to dinner."

"May I hang on to this?" Thomas raised the file on Amanda.

"Of course. Of course. Shall we?" Langston gestured toward the door.

Thomas gave the room and dome another quick scan before following the group out.

***

Part of Thomas had wanted to jump right into his investigation portion of the visit, but quickly realized how tired he was once he was in his room. A quick nap and a shower later, Thomas sat and read the file again as he waited until he would meet the others. The information was basic. Amanda's age. Date of her grandfather's death. The photograph of her grandfather. Her reason for volunteering for the project. Her role as the fifteenth person to participate in the communication part of this project.

Thomas found it surprisingly forthcoming that it mentioned that Amanda was an employee at one of Langston's companies. She wasn't being presented as a medium, just simply as someone who had a strong bond to a deceased relative.

"That's a few points in their favor, I guess." Thomas put the file down.

He heard a knock on his door. Thomas glanced at the time before he walked over and opened the door.

"Hey." Stacey stood in the hallway. "I figured it made more sense if we all walked down together. If that's cool with you." She smiled.

"Yeah. Totally. Let me, uh, make sure I have everything." Thomas shifted awkwardly, not wanting to let the door slam in Stacey's face, but he couldn't hold it open and grab his phone and door key at the same time. "Come in. Sorry." Thomas was frustrated with himself. He had been acting more flustered than he ever had around Stacey. *Get it together.* He shook his head, put his phone in his left pocket, checked that he had his room key in his wallet, and put it in his right pocket. "Ok. Good to go."

Stacey smiled at Thomas as she leaned against the door. "Guess we should get the doctor and head to the lobby."

"Sounds like a plan."

They knocked on Maxwell's door, and, after a moment of waiting for him to gather his things, they went to the lobby.

Langston was waiting for them. "I hope everyone found their rooms comfortable." He clasped his hands together. "If you'll follow me, I will walk us over to the restaurant. Miss Carmichael, I was wondering if I could ask you a few questions about your profession on the way."

Thomas and Maxwell followed a few lengths behind. Stacey looked back at one point and smiled at Thomas.

He returned an almost bashful, wry smile. He let a little laugh out through his nose before looking down.

"So. You wanna tell me about you two?" Maxwell inquired, his voice fairly low. "I've been told I'm an excellent listener." He emphasized "excellent" allowing his self-aware humor to come through.

"I don't know if I can afford you, Doc."

Maxwell laughed. "Well, this one is on the house."

"Alright," Thomas chuckled. "Well, I guess it's pretty obvious that Stace and I used to be together."

"How long ago?"

"Ended about two years ago."

"What happened?"

Thomas shrugged. "She got an offer to be on a major ghost show as a research-er. We have differing opinions on shows like that. I think the sensensationalism does more harm than good. She views those shows, the top tier ones anyway, as a good entry point for people that are interested in the paranormal. At the end of the day, I wasn't going to try to stand in her way if that's what she really wanted. Plus, I mean, I basically make a living off of being a cynical asshole, so maybe she wanted to get away from that. I dunno. Regardless, things just fell apart after that. Our travel sched-ules were completely different. Things like that. Things were never hostile, they just ended."

"Have you dated anyone since then?"

"No." Thomas shook his head.

"Has she?"

"Don't think so. Not as far as I know. And we still have a few mutual friends that love to gossip, so I figure something would have gotten back to me by this point."

Maxwell slowly nodded his head. "Interesting."

"So," Thomas looked at Maxwell, "you have some kind of analysis?"

"Ah. See, the listening is free— it's the analysis that costs the real money." Max-well laughed.

"Oh okay." Thomas laughed as well.

"Besides. It will be a lot more meaningful and impactful when you figure it out for yourself. And you will. Trust me. I'm a doctor."

Thomas laughed through his nose, and nodded in response.

The restaurant was clearly high class, but didn't feel stuffy. It was spacious, with high ceilings. Langston clearly did not like tight spaces in his designs. All the furniture had a handcrafted feel to it, all made of dark elegant wood. The lighting had a soft, orangish yellow glow from the vintage style lightbulbs. A central circular fireplace, though not lit, tied the room together. Everything about the design felt comforting.

They all took a seat at a roomy square table. Stacey sat across from Thomas, with Langston on his left, and Maxwell on his right.

One female server, and two chefs, who Thomas could see in the open kitchen, had been brought in to work the evening.

"Our food will start arriving shortly," Langston spoke after they had all been seated. "In the meantime, a good drink while we wait? Thomas, I believe you are a fan of bourbon and whiskey, if I recall correctly."

"You've definitely done your research," Thomas replied.

"Excellent!" Langston turned to the server, "Liz, bring the bottle of Whistle Pig twelve year, and four...?" He looked at everyone, who all nodded in response, "four glasses."

"Is the Whistle Pig to help influence a favorable report?" Thomas let the words out without thinking.

Stacey looked at Thomas, her eyes wide in a *don't say stuff like that* look.

Maxwell cringed just a bit and tried not to laugh at the awkwardness.

"I have also learned that you lean into skepticism and incredulity." Langston laughed, clearly not put off by Thomas's comment. "I find it fascinating that some- one that expounds on the reality of the non-physical realm has... doubled down on those traits."

Liz returned with the rye whiskey. She began to pour a glass for each of them.

"I mean," Thomas paused, "I personally feel that's what makes me a good re- searcher and paranormal investigator. Thank you." He acknowledged Liz, and then picked up his glass to take a sip. "Not every bump in the night is a ghost or goblin. I think it's my skepticism and incredulity that adds to my credibility. For better or worse."

"So what would it take to convince you?" Langston asked in all seriousness as he took a sip.

"That's the thing." Thomas pursed his lips slightly and shook his head. "There isn't one specific piece of evidence that I'm looking for. It's one of those 'I know it when I see it' kind of things. I mean, the vast majority of cases I've been involved in turn out to be something mundane and grounded. Whether it be misidentification, deception on the part of either the witness, or someone tricking the witness. Things like that."

"If you had to put a number on it, how many cases would say are false claims?" Langston took another sip.

"I mean, I'm estimating here, but I'd say..." Thomas scrunched his nose in thought. "Ninety eight percent?"

"Really?" Langston raised his eyebrows in surprise. "That high?"

Thomas nodded.

"What about the other two percent?" Langston continued.

Thomas shrugged. "Those are cases where I couldn't find any form of alternative explanation, deception, or I had some very clear experience or evidence that it was indeed a paranormal event of some kind."

"This makes me even more glad I asked you all here." Langston smiled. "I feel I am learning so much more about this whole world. The approach in how you investigate and make your determinations is fascinating in and of itself."

Food had begun to arrive at the table.

"I know Griff and I have always tried to make sure clients know we might not give answers they want to hear," Stacey added. "So what happens if the three of us recommend you stop your experiments?"

"Then we shut that part down and run everything like a normal resort," Langston stated matter of factly. "This resort is still built to function in the same capacity, and with the same mission statement, regardless of the supernatural aspect. I didn't become wealthy by being a bad businessman with no alternative plans." Langston laughed. "It's still a beautiful and special location, with a perfect balance of natural seclusion and state-of-the-art amenities."

"You mentioned before about this being a special, or perfect, location, or something like that, earlier today too. What do you mean by that?" Stacey inquired.

"Well. Beyond just how beautiful the land is here, which I suppose I've already made that point enough, this particular spot is either on, or near, ley lines, as well as large deposits of limestone in the area."

Stacey and Thomas shared a quick look, both cocking their heads and squinting their eyes as they processed the new information.

"Again, theoretically," Langston continued for Maxwell's benefit, "ley lines are like spiritual rivers, if you will, with concentrated pockets of spiritual energy along the way. Limestone can store spiritual energy, which could amplify the effect. Those aspects would then make it easier for spirit energy to come through. Plus, I believe, the general spiritual... mood, I suppose, will help people find their peace and aid in the resolution of their grief."

"I did want to ask about that." Maxwell finally spoke. "The other stuff is clearly out of my range of expertise, but regardless of real or not, while I can certainly see the benefits of having a... relatively tangible representation of their lost loved one, I can also see it having the opposite effect. Instead of letting go, they could become more attached. Wanting to constantly summon their loved one and communicate. Could see it becoming an addiction. Or any number of possible negative consequences."

"It is something to consider." Langston processed his thoughts. "I do share your concerns about individuals wanting to use this as a way to 'video chat' with loved ones they've lost, which is not my intent. I mean, once one of our volunteers has made contact, we do not have them do it again. But even from this brief conversation, I am seeing there may be various new ethical issues to consider." Langston smiled. "But this is one of the reasons I wanted all of you here."

"So, if you don't mind my asking," Maxwell continued, "have you tried to make contact yourself?"

"No. I haven't yet."

"May I ask why?"

Langston nodded, and his mood turned more somber. "One reason is that I have tried to make sure this project isn't just about me. I clearly have a personal interest in all of this working, and I believe my experience gives me an understanding of what others have, and are, going through. I truly want to help people. And by having others go through the process before I do, kind of forces and ensures that I don't make this all about me. And, I suppose, there may be a part of me that isn't ready to let go or face my grief just yet." Langston smiled sadly. He broke eye contact for the first time and started to drift into his own thoughts.

There was an all too long few seconds of silence before Stacey pulled things back.

"Well, regardless of anything else, this place is beautiful. And this food is incredible! How are you handling supply with the resort's remote location?"

Thomas took another sip of whiskey and listened to Langston, who was back to his energetic self, explain his mission of only buying from local farmers, and his various purchasing and hiring habits. Thomas admired Stacey's ability to pull conversations out of any form of a nosedive. He was pretty sure he would have just sat there awkwardly until Langston changed the subject.

As dinner had begun to wrap up, Alice arrived to make sure the trio had her contact information for when they devised their plan.

"Well," Langston looked at his watch, "I need to call my grandchildren before it gets too late. So I will bid you all a good evening." He stood. "Oh, and take the bottle with you. A gift, not a bribe." He laughed. "I'm happy to share good whiskey with those who appreciate it."

They all thanked Langston, who said goodnight again before leaving.

Alice, after making sure she had everything she needed from them, took her leave as well.

The trio looked at each other.

"Shall we?" Thomas nodded toward the door.

They agreed, each taking their glass, and Thomas the bottle of rye, with them.

The three convened in Thomas's room, and Thomas poured another glass of whiskey for each of them.

"So. Initial thoughts?" Thomas inquired.

"So far, our host seems sincere in what he's telling us," responded Stacey. "Granted, we are still dealing with first impressions, but Langston seems sincere."

"I would agree with that." Maxwell took a sip of whiskey. "He seemed pretty honest about his grieving process, or lack thereof. And he does seem to legitimately want to use this place to help people. But, I suppose there's also a chance he's putting on an act and lying."

"That's always a possibility, unfortunately," Stacey agreed. "Assuming he is being honest, what are some things we should keep in mind?"

Thomas leaned back and gathered his thoughts. "Doc. You referred to what we saw as a seance and ouija board earlier."

"Yeah."

"That has me thinking we should definitely bear in mind that Langston could be the one being deceived. One of the major blemishes on the Spiritualism movement was mediums and such committing fraud. Tricking people out of their money with the promise of communication with the dead. They'd rig devices to make knocks, blow out candles, make curtains billow, ectoplasm appear, and all that. This could very well be a high tech version of that."

Stacey nodded. "Get yourself in good with a wealthy vulnerable person and take them for a ride."

"Exactly." Thomas took another drink.

"Makes sense." Stacey nodded.

Maxwell listened to the brief exchange. "I'm definitely going to be the weak link here, so the more we get into all the ghost stuff, you are gonna have to explain it to me like I don't know anything. Assume I'm dumb."

"Oh, Griff will have no problem doing that," Stacey teased.

Maxwell laughed.

Thomas gestured incredulously and let out a laugh. "I mean. You're not wrong, but jeez."

They spent some time planning out what they needed to get done the next day. Interviews, file and video review, closer inspection of the dome, among other things. Once they had finalized their list, Thomas texted it to Alice. A few moments later, her response came back.

"Ok." Thomas began reading the text. "She says she'll have everything arranged, and she will make sure we get what we need if anything else comes up. Cool. I'll just text her thanks. Sweet. Looks like we are good to go."

"Well." Maxwell slapped his hands down on his thighs and stood up. "I think I need some sleep. So, if you will excuse me, I will see you both in the morning."

"Night, Doc." Thomas gave a small two finger salute.

"Goodnight," Stacey said.

Maxwell performed a slight bow with a flourish of his hand, and then left the room.

Stacey handed her glass to Thomas, who split the remaining whiskey between them, and handed the glass back to Stacey.

"Here's to a good day of investigating." Stacey raised her glass.

"I'll drink to that." Thomas clinked his glass against Stacey's.

"You'd drink to anything, Griff," Stacey teased.

"Again, also true." Thomas laughed. He was feeling more relaxed than he had been at the start of the day. Some mixture of the alcohol, and the familiar feeling of planning out an investigation with Stacey.

"So, uh, how's the show going?"

"It's good," Stacey responded. "I'm not as hands-on in the actual 'investigation' side of things like when we worked together, but I get paid to travel the world, read, and do research, so I can't complain. How about you?"

"Mostly freelance work. A few guest speaking engagements. Been trying to write a book on paranormal research, but that's been slow going."

"Sounds like you've had a lot going on."

"Yeah. Been trying to keep busy. Never any shortage of claims of the paranormal, so that helps."

"That's the truth." Stacey chuckled. "Hey. We have a big day tomorrow, so we should probably get some sleep."

Thomas nodded in agreement. "Yeah. You're probably right."

Stacey smiled, stood up, and made her way to the door.

Thomas followed and held the door open behind Stacey.

Stacey stepped into the hallway and turned around. "It's really good seeing you."

"You too." Thomas smiled.

"Goodnight, Griff."

"Goodnight, Stace." Thomas leaned against the door, lost in thought as Stacey went to her room. He heard her door shut, and let out a sigh. Thomas slowly shut the door to his room.

It wasn't long before he was in bed and asleep.

Thomas woke up a bit groggy, but otherwise surprisingly rested, given the alcohol and unfamiliar bed. He took a shower, got dressed, then headed outside to take a walk.

There was no denying the beauty of the place. Thomas felt predominately relaxed as he walked around and took in fresh air. As a place to stay in order to remove yourself from the troubles of the world, and start to let things go, Thomas felt it worked. There was something Thomas couldn't quite pinpoint though. Like the tiniest of itches in the back of his mind. He passed it off as a small case of nerves, and drinking a little too much, but he took note of the feeling anyway.

By the time Thomas arrived back at the lobby, breakfast had been laid out by Alice and an employee of the resort. The smell of food and coffee was like olfactory heaven to Thomas.

"I was just about to text you that we had food down here for you," Alice said.. "I'll have the conference room ready for your interview with Amanda. If there are any issues with access to anything, just let me know, and I will take care of it. And just let me know when you all want lunch"

"Thanks, Alice. Really appreciate your help with everything."

She shook her head. "My pleasure. And my job." Alice laughed.

"Fair enough." Thomas chuckled.

"Anyway, just let me know."

"Will do."

Thomas relaxed, ate some food, and sipped his coffee. He looked up as Stacey approached.

"Good morning, Griff."

"Morning, Stace."

Stacey sat down and poured herself a coffee.

Maxwell soon joined the others.

"Mornin,' Doc," Thomas greated Maxwell as he sat down.

"Good morning."

"How'd you sleep?" Stacey asked.

"Like a baby." Maxwell tossed a couple of grapes into his mouth.

Thomas made a face. "So you woke up every few hours scream-crying?"

Maxwell laughed. "Pretty much."

After breakfast, the trio walked over to the resort headquarters and made their way to the conference room.

"So, I'm thinking you should take the lead on the interview, Griff," Stacey suggested. "Figure if things get defensive, I can jump in and play good cop or whatever you want to call it."

"Works for me."

Everyone agreed to the plan.

Amanda arrived soon after.

Thomas sat at one end of the table, facing the door, while Stacey and Maxwell sat to his right and left, respectively. Amanda took a seat across from Thomas. The seating arrangement was specific to make sure the interviewee did not feel trapped or defensive.

Everyone shared "good mornings" and they were ready to begin.

"We really appreciate you coming in to talk with us," Thomas said.

"Of course!"

"How'd you get involved with this project?"

"Well, I work for one of Mr. Langston's companies, and I had been going to a counselor the company provides. Part of their 'Whole Person Health and Wellness' initiative. I guess they asked several people if they wanted to participate in the counseling experiment, or whatever you want to call it. I said yes, obviously."

"If you don't mind going into it, what exactly were the circumstances around your grandfather's death?"

Amanda nodded. "I was away on an internship overseas. I knew grandpa was sick, but it took a major turn for the worse. I was going to come home, but everyone insisted that's not what grandpa wanted. He wanted me to focus on my future. Still… I can't help but feel, I don't know, guilty? Like I was being selfish? Everyone told me I made the right decision in staying, but I guess I didn't believe it. Or at least feel it."

"What are your beliefs when it comes to the afterlife and the paranormal?"

"I mean, I've always felt there was something after, you know? Not sure I'd say I believed in ghosts, if that's what you mean. After yesterday, I definitely think there's something after we die."

Thomas nodded.

The conversation moved from the current topic to Amanda's history and interests. Personal questions helped give a comparison of reaction and body language.

They wrapped up the interview and thanked Amanda for her time.

After Amanda had left the room, Thomas turned to Stacey.

"So, what do you think, Stace?"

"She seems pretty genuine to me. If it's all fake, I don't think she's in on it."

Thomas nodded.

"Doc?"

"I'm not an expert on body language, but I can usually tell when someone is holding something back. And I didn't pick up on that with her."

"Yeah," Thomas sighed. "I came to the same conclusion."

"You sound strangely disappointed with her honesty." Maxwell looked confused.

"It's because we usually start with the premise that a claim is false," Stacey responded. "If we can pick up on deception, or catch a witness in an outright lie, it makes our jobs easier. If Amanda had been lying, then boom, we have a strong case already that this is all a ruse. But, we all think she's being honest, so that means we still don't know what exactly is going on. Granted, she might be an amazing actress, but I don't think that's the case."

"That makes a lot of sense actually." Maxwell crossed his arms and leaned back in his chair. "So what's next, boss?" He looked at Thomas.

"Boss," Thomas said thoughtfully. "I like that." He nodded his head in joking approval. "Well, I'd like to take a closer look at the dome, and start on the videos of the experiments. I'm thinking I'd get started on that while you two interview Sinister Steve."

"Griff. That's kinda mean," Stacey laughingly admonished Thomas.

"Am I wrong?"

"I mean. No."

"Nicknames?" Maxwell interjected. "I want a cool nickname."

"I already call you 'Doc'."

"Yeah, but I have a PhD. Seems kinda obvious."

"I mean, I could call you 'Maxy-Waxy' if you want."

Maxwell looked a little grossed out. "Doc's fine."

"Oh my god." Stacey had her head down in her hand, in amused exasperation. "Anyway." She dragged out each syllable. "The plan sounds good. Probably a lot of video to go through, so let's get done with what we need to, and reconvene as soon as we can."

"Alright. Let's do it." Thomas stood up from the table.

Stacey and Maxwell went to go talk to DiAngelo as Thomas made his way to the control room and the mini dome.

"Hi!" The female tech from yesterday turned and looked up from her work. "Mr. Griffin, right? I'm Michelle."

"Nice to meet you, Michelle. Officially." Thomas shook Michelle's outstretched hand. "And please, call me Thomas."

"Sure thing! So, I was told to show you whatever you needed, and to answer any of your questions. Where do you want to start?"

"You seem super happy about being my guide this morning."

Michelle laughed. "I get a little over enthusiastic about discussing technology in general, and I haven't really been able to discuss any of this with anyone. NDAs and all that, so I guess it's all been so pent up!"

Thomas laughed. "Fair enough." Thomas looked through the window at the dome. "Maybe let's start there?"

"Follow me!"

After entering the room, Thomas searched for anything that might be projecting the image they saw into the dome. The only electronics he found were the speakers hanging from the wall, and the cameras that were used to document the tests. He couldn't find any evidence of hidden projectors, so he pushed that possibility to the bottom of the list.

Thomas turned his attention to the dome. He circled the outside and inspected it. He stepped inside and looked for any evidence of projection devices. The only external electronics attached to the dome were two thin microphones that were connected to the soundboard in the observation room. He was leaning even more toward the theory that the dome itself was a hologram projector of some sorts.

"So, uh, how does this all work?" Thomas gestured around the dome. He stepped out of it and looked at Michelle, who stepped forward.

"Well, the glass itself is based on the same principle as smart glass. In regular smart glass, an electric current causes the liquid crystals to line up, allowing transparency. When the current is turned off, the crystals randomize, scattering the light, which causes the opaqueness. This glass is a specific collection and arrangement of crystals that, when the power is on, allow the energy to build to make it easier for the spirit forms that we've seen to manifest."

"Where's the electricity connected?"

"That comes from the base, here." She touched the covered, rectangular base panels. "It sends the power up through the connecting rods." She touched the silvery cylinders. "Which then power the panels."

"Why does it look like something is flowing in the rods?"

"That's the mercury in the outer casing. It's supposed to help keep the spirits contained. Basically, I was given the parameters, and it was my job to make it work. I was given the specific geometric alignment, or symbol, the crystals in the glass are supposed to make, and I was told which materials to incorporate. Something to do with which crystals and such are conducive to spiritual energy." Michelle shrugged slightly. "I made it work. The science aspect of generating EMF and lining up crystals with electricity I get. Obviously. As to the supernatural side of things," Michelle paused. "I know this probably sounds ridiculous, but I don't know why it works. It just does."

"Who gave you the specs on what you needed to do?"

"That all came from DiAngelo. His concept, my creation, I guess."

"Probably should have asked this before walking inside of it, but it's not on right now is it?"

"Oh, no. We make sure it's off when we aren't testing it. Basically, the procedure is to let it warm up an hour before use, make sure it's humming, and then shut it down immediately once we are done."

"So. Do *you* believe in ghosts?"

Michelle laughed. "I didn't before this project. Now? I mean, I can't really argue with what I've seen."

"Fair enough." Thomas turned to Michelle. "Every test gets filmed right?"

"Correct. We have all that archived on the computers."

"Can we?"

"Of course!"

They left the room and went back to the control room. Michelle pulled up the directory with all the digital footage of the tests.

"Everything is there. It's a lot though."

"Does anyone rewatch these?"

"Not really. They're mostly there for documentation, and liability I guess. Even though we have everyone sign a waiver, along with the NDA."

"Is there any way you could copy or get me remote access to these? I have my laptop back in my room. It'll be easier to go through the video that way for me." He started to explain having proper video playback programs and such, but Michelle laughed, and waved him off.

"It's all good! Alice told me to get you whatever you needed, and she speaks for Mr. Langston, so…"

"I appreciate it."

"What else do you think you'll need, off the top of your head?"

"Uh, the files on the test subjects, and the schematics on the dome, if possible."

"Sure! So the files are all old school analog, so if you want to come with me to my office, we can grab a drive, and then get the files."

It didn't take long, and soon they were back in the control room. Michelle began transferring the video files, while Thomas thumbed through a few of the paper documents.

Michelle handed Thomas the folder she had been carrying.

"This is the hard copy of the specs and parameters for the panels and the dome. I'm copying the digital file as well."

"This is awesome. Thank you."

"No problem!"

Michelle turned and waved in greeting at Stacey and Maxwell as they walked into the room and went to check on the file transfer.

"Hey," Stacey greeted Thomas.

"Hey," Thomas replied. "How'd it go?"

"It was certainly interesting."

Maxwell made a *you can say that again* face.

Thomas scrunched his face in thought for a second. "Michelle."

"Yeah?"

"How long have you known DiAngelo?"

"Only since the beginning of the project. Think I met him a few days after I was brought in."

"What's your personal opinion of him?" Thomas continued. "If you don't mind us asking."

"Off the record?"

"Yeah."

"I mean, he kind of gives me the heebie-jeebies, if I'm being honest. Not like full on creeper status, but there is definitely something off about him." Michelle looked back at the monitor. "Looks like everything is done copying." She disconnected the drive and handed it to Thomas. "Oh, and I guess in case you all think of anything else you need, just text me." She scribbled her number down on a piece of paper and gave it to Thomas. "I usually work pretty late, so whatever you all need."

The trio thanked Michelle, took the files and drive, and went back to Thomas's room.

Alice had the food for their lunch brought there, so they could eat while they worked.

"So, give me the scoop. What happened with the interview?" Thomas inquired between sips of sweet tea.

"Well," Stacey began, "he certainly likes showing off his collection of various busts of gods of the underworld and death. Usual suspects like Anubis and Osiris. Charon imagery. Stuff like that."

"So bordering on the try-too-hard-to-show-he's-an-expert side of things?"

"That's what we thought too. Adds to the charlatan theory. He also gave off a kind of a used car salesman, cult leader type vibe. Lots of books sitting out on spiritualism, sacred geometry, the occult. Not automatically strange, but given the context…"

"Right…" Thomas nodded. "How'd he get involved?"

"Apparently Langston contacted him," Maxwell answered. "DiAngelo has been doing his 'finding a bridge between the two worlds' thing for two decades. So kind of a match made in heaven— DiAngelo's theories and Langston's financial backing. And remember how I said I could usually tell if someone was holding something back?"

"Yeah?"

"Definitely holding something back."

"Well," Thomas scratched at his beard, "let's see if we can figure out what that is."

Thomas and Stacey started with looking at the schematics for the dome, and would move to the videos after that, while Maxwell started with the participant files.

The schematics showed the specific geometric formation the crystals required. It had taken a multitude of tests to find the right power levels and adjustments to get the desired formation. After a bit of searching, the formation did seem to be based on various summoning circles and spiritual gateways in the realm of sacred geometry. There was still the possibility that the dome functioned as a complex LCD display system, creating a hologram image, but this was strange, as both Thomas and Stacey thought.

Video analysis was slow, as it always was. Pouring over the images, freezing and advancing frame by frame, listening for anything out of the ordinary. Thomas and Stacey were used to it, but it was a time consuming process, especially to do it right.

The videos showed the development of failed attempts, to the beginnings of faint glows of energy, to the eventual manifestations. Thomas hadn't found any evidence of projection yet. He had a theory that the panels somehow were oriented in such a way that the crystal formation, in proper alignment, would make the images appear. But that would make DiAngelo some sort of technical genius to be able to hide that within the premise of sacred geometry imagery. It was still possible that Michelle was in on it, so he couldn't rule it out, but the theory was starting to fall apart.

Evening was upon them. They had been at it for hours. And even with taking short breaks, it was getting exhausting. Thomas had his eyes fixed on the screen, when he finally noticed something. Something odd in the glowing energy as it took shape into the form of the deceased. He went back a few frames, paused, zoomed in, and advanced frame by frame.

"What?" Thomas mumbled under his breath as he squinted and looked closer at the image on his screen.

"Hey! I want you two to listen to this." Stacey had removed her headphones and called Thomas and Maxwell over.

"You first." She handed the headphones to Maxwell. "I want you to listen to it and write down what you think you hear. Don't say anything, just listen, and then write it down. I'll replay it as many times as you need."

Maxwell nodded, and put on the headphones. He listened intently. After several listens, he handed the headphones to Thomas, and sat down to write what he heard.

Thomas put the headphones on and nodded to Stacey. He was confused by what he heard. There was no way.

"Play it again." He listened very carefully and shook his head. "One more time." He took the headphones off and looked at Stacey. "There's no way."

She nodded excitedly. "Write it down though!"

Thomas quickly wrote down what he heard.

"Alright! You two ready?" She gestured with the notebook she had in her hands. "You first." Stacey pointed at Maxwell.

"I think I heard, 'we are coming, from the void we cry?' maybe?"

Stacey and Thomas tossed their notebooks on the table.

Maxwell looked at both, which read "We are coming. From the void we rise."

"I was close," Maxwell commented. "So what does that mean?"

"The Toolie case," Thomas answered Maxwell, but was engaged more in conversation with Stacey.

"It's insane, right!" Stacey responded excitedly. "Like, I know that could have been planted for us to find, but this is from a test over six months before we were asked in. That would be a serious long con."

"So… what's the Toolie case?" Maxwell was still confused.

"You remember that two percent that Thomas mentioned?"

"Uh huh."

"Well that was one of them."

"Long story short," Thomas interjected, "we found evidence of an inhuman haunt that I couldn't explain away, including a voice that said that same phrase."

"I can probably figure out what that means, but explain." Maxwell pointed at himself. "Remember, talk to me like I'm dumb."

Stacey laughed. "Right. Sorry. So. There are two major types of hauntings that are generally accepted by the community. Residual and intelligent. Residual is like playback of past events. You can't interact with them, it's just like watching a home movie or something."

"So like," Maxwell thought for a second, "seeing a Civil War soldier walking across the battlefield."

"Exactly. Intelligent haunts, on the other hand, you can interact with. You can get responses, or see the entity doing different things. In that category you have human and inhuman. Human, as is probably obvious, is the spirit or energy of a deceased person. Inhuman, however, is everything else. Could be a manifestation of negative energy that's essentially been given life by a person. Demons. Interdimensional beings. All kinds of possibilities."

"So that voice could be the same inhuman haunt spirit that you two heard in that other case."

"Yeah." Stacey nodded. "If so, it's a huge find. And kind of scary, honestly."

"Given that context," Thomas moved over to his laptop, "I want you all to look at this."

Stacey and Maxwell gathered behind Thomas to look at the screen.

"So, it's only there for a frame, but…" Thomas advanced the image by tapping the forward arrow. "There."

Within the energy, and right before it took the appearance of the requested deceased, a twisted figure appeared. The figure's body was made up of faces, all twisted, stretched, and tangled around each other. The entity's own face was blank and distorted, almost appeared to be, or surrounded in, thick vines. The body seemed to extrude short, but defined, tendrils that, based on the blur on the image, were moving.

"What is that?" Maxwell was equal parts shocked and confused.

"I've never seen anything like that before." Stacey was in awe.

Thomas exhaled through his nose, and shook his head. "I mean, it could be matrixing, but I don't think so. Especially given that voice you found."

"So this is all real," Maxwell still spoke in disbelief.

"It's looking that way," Thomas answered. "But they obviously aren't calling up what Langston thinks they're calling up."

"Not at all," Stacey agreed.

"I mean, it could still be an elaborate hoax, but either way, they need to shut things down." Thomas looked at Stacey and laughed in disbelief.

"It's amazing you found those." Maxwell leaned in again to get a closer look at the image on the screen. "I can see why you two are so meticulous."

"I'm a little surprised I caught the voice," Stacey said. "It was pretty low, and hidden in the humming sound that's in all the videos."

"Do either one of you have a signal in here?" Thomas held up his phone. "I'm trying to text Alice about our findings, but it won't send."

Stacey and Maxwell checked and found they didn't have a signal either.

"Alright. I'm gonna step outside and see if I can send this text."

The sun had almost disappeared, and darkness soon took over. The air was still, but Thomas felt something was off. He looked at his phone. Still no signal. The message wouldn't send.

"Damn it."

"Phone won't work?"

"Shit!" Thomas flinched, startled by Alice's voice.

"Sorry!" She almost laughed. "I didn't mean to sneak up on you like that. I've been trying to text you, but can't get a signal, so I figured I'd just walk over."

"Yeah." Thomas lifted his phone. "Was trying to text you too. But nothing."

"Never had any issues before. It's strange."

"Well, I'm glad you walked down here 'cause…" Thomas's voice trailed off. "Hum. The humming!"

Alice shook her head, confused.

"I'm an idiot. The dome. It literally hums when it's on. We need to grab the others."

Alice followed Thomas to his room. Stacey and Maxwell looked up from their work as Thomas barged in.

"I think we have a problem."

"What's going on, Griff?" Stacey looked concerned.

"That big dome? I think it's been running for a while. Building energy. If what we saw could come through in the little dome after only an hour of being on…"

"Something bigger, or a lot of things, could come through." Stacey finished the sentence.

"This is bad, isn't it?" Maxwell looked like he had indigestion.

"Will somebody please explain what's going on?" Alice asked with concern in her voice.

"Short version? Evil spirits might come through portals that are being opened in the domes," Thomas said.

"Come again?" Alice couldn't believe what she heard.

"We need to move." Thomas turned back to Stacey and Maxwell. "If we don't get the big dome shut down, I'm afraid something really bad is going to happen."

"Let's go then." Stacey stood.

The four headed out of the hotel and toward the large dome. As they got closer, they could see a blue glow breaking the natural dark of night.

"Wait!" Maxwell halted the group. "We need to get out of sight."

The group saw what caused Maxwell to stop. A robed figure stood guard at the entrance of the dome. Other figures stood in a semi circle inside toward the center of the dome, facing inward. Another figure stood, arms outstretched, in front of the collection of robed figures, all facing the large blue ovoid-like shape of energy.

The four hunched down behind a planter box. Thomas sank down, his back against the panels of cedar. Maxwell continued to peer over, keeping a lookout, while Stacey and Alice discussed something.

"What's the plan, boss?" Maxwell didn't break his gaze from the bizarre scene.

Thomas looked back over the planter at the dome. Featureless entities had begun to emerge from the rift. They were mostly humanoid in shape, though freakishly elongated. Their almond shaped heads balanced on long, thin necks. Spindly arms and hands reached down well past where their waists should have been. There were no limbs extending from the torso, which tapered off and looked ripped and shredded at the bottom. Each entity, in turn, flowed around behind a robed figure. Once an entity was in position, its long, needle-like fingers penetrated their chosen cultist between their neck and shoulders. As the entity did this, the host cultist spasmed in some apparent mix of pain and ecstasy before settling and becoming expressionless. The shredded ends of the entity's torso merged into the lower back of the cultist, giving the appearance of some grotesque piggyback ride.

"I have an idea," Thomas shook his head, baffled by what he was witnessing, "but it really hinges on Michelle still working with us. And not being part of that."

"While you boys do that, Alice and I are going to go get Mr. Langston," Stacey informed Thomas. "I know you don't like to split the party, Griff," Stacey raised her hand to cut off Thomas's objection before he could start, "but it will be easier for you two to sneak into the offices than a group of four. Plus, I have my own plan, but I need to get something."

Thomas clenched his jaw, but, based on what they were seeing, there didn't seem to be much time to waste arguing or having a deep discussion about details.

"Be careful, huh?" Thomas resigned himself to the plan.

"Of course." Stacey winked to reassure Thomas.

"0451." Alice handed Thomas one of her key cards. "My code and key works for all the locks on site."

"Thanks."

Stacey and Alice moved quickly toward their destination.

Thomas looked at Maxwell, who still kept an eye on the dome.

"Ready?"

Maxwell pulled a cross out of his pocket. "Yup."

"Wouldn't have taken you as the religious type, Doc."

"Well, figure now's as good a time as any to start. My grandmother gave it to me as a gift. Kind of an 'in case of emergency' type thing. Pretty sure this counts."

"Fair enough." Thomas chuckled. "Let's move."

The two men stayed low, moving from cover to cover as speedily as they could.

They finally reached the back door. Thomas, while Maxwell kept an eye behind them, quickly punched 0451 into the keypad, and swiped the keycard. A very brief moment passed, though feeling like an anxious minute, and the door unlocked, allowing the two men inside.

They jogged somewhat stealthily down the hallway to Michelle's office, which had regular light spilling out from the doorway.

Thomas peeked his head around the doorframe and saw Michelle sitting at her desk, engrossed in paperwork.

Thomas knocked on the open door. "Hey. Michelle."

She dropped her pen, startled. "Oh my god. You scared the shit out of me." She laughed it off. "What's up?"

"We need your help with something." Thomas and Maxwell entered the office.

"Totally!"

"So. The, uh, big dome is on, and there are, uh, entities coming through the portal it's opened."

"What?" Michelle was in shock. "It's on? We weren't even supposed to start testing it until at least another two weeks. Who turned it on?"

"My guess? DiAngelo. Don't know for sure, but, I mean, I do know there are things manifesting like crazy, and we need to stop it."

"I mean, yeah! What do you need me to do?"

"It's a theory, but I need you to figure out the exact inverse of the pattern used for the summoning. As quickly as possible. Please."

"Yeah. I can, I can totally figure that out. We'll need to go to the control room, so I can see the display."

Michelle led them to the control room and began setting up.

"Might be a stupid question, but why don't we just cut the power to the dome?" Maxwell asked Thomas. "You know. Shut the whole thing down."

"Nah, that's a good question. If they are coming through that particular gate, simply closing it means whatever's already crossed through is stuck on this side. Blocking the pathway will make it that much more difficult to send them back. So what I'm thinking, since a specific geometric pattern was used to help pull them through, I'm theorizing that inverting the pattern will help push them back."

"So changing the settings from suck, to blow. Or, I guess, the reverse of that."

Thomas furrowed his brow, processing what Maxwell said. "Yeah. I mean. Either would work really, depending on your perspective, I guess." He shook his head. "Anyway. My hope is that the pattern inversion, plus a dash of exorcism, will drive them back to where they came from."

"So you think they're demons?"

"Demons. Interdimensional beings. No idea really. I just know spirits of ill intent get repelled when faced with powers of good. And I'm assuming those things are not good, given the secrecy, their appearance, people in cultist robes, and the whole apparent possession thing."

"Makes sense." Maxwell nodded.

"I'm worried about containment though. Need to give Michelle enough time to figure out the right pattern. When those things get out, who knows what they're gonna do."

"Probably not setting up a spirit zoo," Maxwell paused. "Man. Never thought I'd say those two words together. What a difference two days makes."

Thomas snapped his figures. "I have an idea! Michelle, do you need any help from us?"

"I mean, I'm all set up, but it might be faster with someone helping me observe the changes and make the comparison. Plus, not gonna lie, I'm a little, uh, freaked out from the conversation that was just happening."

"Fair. Doc, you got this?"

"Sure thing." Maxwell nodded "Wait? Where are you going?"

"To the restaurant."

"Evil spirit invasion got you hungry?" Maxwell was genuinely confused.

"Kind of, actually. But no. I need, like, a shit ton of salt. Michelle. Where's the control for the big dome?"

Michelle had spun her seat toward Thomas and Maxwell. "There's a small separate building on the back left of the dome, if you are facing the main entrance."

"Meet you two there then?" Thomas looked at Michelle and Maxwell.

"Sounds good," Michelle and Maxwell agreed.

Thomas left them to their work and exited the building. A quick glance at the dome showed that more of the featureless beings had emerged from the ovoid. It seemed to be slow going, however, thankfully for Thomas. He went as quickly as he could, on the most direct route he dared, until he was sure he was out of sight of the guard, and broke into a run.

He arrived at the front door of the restaurant, out of breath. He yanked on the door, which resisted his attempt to open it. Thomas looked down, and saw it was locked with a traditional bolt and key.

"You gotta be kidding me."

He panted and grimaced, trying to get his breath back.

"Back door. Gotta be a back door."

He pushed himself to run around to the right and behind the building. The door there had a keypad and card slider. Code. Key. The door unlocked.

"Thank God."

Thomas entered what he assumed was the manager's office, which he promptly moved through and out the office door and began searching for the kitchen. He kept his eye out for dry storage, but he figured he'd see if it was attached to the kitchen first. His recollection of where the server had brought the food led him to the main dining area, and to the double doors leading to the kitchen.

There were two doors at the back of the kitchen. One led to the walk-in freezer and cooler, and another to dry storage. Thomas entered the storage room and began his search for salt. The storage was well organized, but the adrenaline, lightheadedness from sprinting, and his general level of panic all made it difficult for him to focus.

"Get it together, Griffin," he admonished himself. He took a moment to refocus. Thomas resumed his search of the shelves and found several five pound plastic containers of salt. He grabbed two off the shelf when he heard voices, muffled from the other side of the door.

"In there," one of the voices said.

The door swung open. Thomas spun and raised his fists, still clenching the salt containers.

"Griff?"

"Stace?" Thomas lowered his hand and let his head drop in relief.

"Looks like we had the same idea."

Thomas raised the salt containers. "Great minds, right?"

"I had to go get my book," Stacey gestured with the leather bound text she had in her hand, "and then we got Langston." She walked over to Thomas. "Do you have the prayer memorized?" Stacey asked, impressed.

Thomas paused for a moment. He now remembered that phones weren't working, and he wouldn't have been able to look it up.

"I was just gonna ask nicely."

"That would probably work just as well." Stacey smiled sincerely, and helped Thomas grab more salt containers off the shelf.

They returned to the kitchen, where Alice and Langston were waiting, and set the eight containers on the prep table. After unscrewing the lids, Stacey began blessing the salt.

"Almighty God, we ask you to bless this salt, as once you blessed the salt scattered over the water by the prophet Elisha. Wherever this salt is sprinkled, drive away the power of evil, and protect us always by the presence of your Holy Spirit. Grant this through Christ our Lord. Amen."

She went two at a time, laying her hands over the open mouth of the containers.

Thomas stood back by Alice and Langton.

"I can't believe all this is happening." Langston was distraught. "It's my fault really. So fixated on the goal, I never considered these consequences."

"Look," Thomas was understanding, but firm, "there will be plenty of time for lamenting and hand-wringing over hubris later on, but we need to stay focused on fixing this right now."

Langston nodded. "You're right." He took a deep breath, and straightened his shoulders. "Me moping about isn't going to change anything." His resolve was returning. "So what are we going to do?"

"Well," Thomas took a breath, "we need to get rid of that guard first if we are going to make the salt ring around the dome."

"I have a plan for that," Alice chimed in. "I'll be right back." She swiftly exited the kitchen.

Thomas and Langston waited in silence as Stacey finished up with the salt.

"All done."

Thomas helped Stacey screw the caps back onto the containers.

Alice returned just as they were finishing the last ones.

"Ready when you are." Alice looked at everyone.

Thomas and Stacey looked at each other and nodded.

Thomas picked up two containers in each hand. "Let's do this."

***

"Excuse me, sir!" Langston shouted with all the confidence he could muster at the person standing guard. "What are you doing on my property? I demand to speak to you at once."

The robed figure looked at Langston, and then approached. The cultist took long, determined strides, closing the distance rapidly.

"Now. What is this all about?" Langston demanded, the person now about ten feet away.

Alice leaped out of hiding, jamming her crackling stun gun against the robed figure's side.

The cultist attempted to turn their seizing, pain riddled body toward Alice.

Thomas ran up from the side, and kicked out the person's legs.

Alice reapplied the stun gun, making sure it had enough contact to be effective, while Thomas used the zip ties Alice had retrieved to bind the cultist's ankles and wrists.

They looked down at the man. He was still in a spasm, and had clearly thrown up.

"Think you used enough zip ties?" Alice remarked, having seen Thomas use an exuberant number to bind the cultist.

"Better safe than sorry." Thomas shrugged. "Good thing you had that," He nodded toward the stun gun.

"Always have it on me in case of emergencies. And other things." Alice let off two crackling sparks.

Thomas looked confused and concerned.

"We can spice things up in the bedroom later, Griff." Stacey bumped shoulders with Thomas. "But let's get this circle done first, eh?"

"Right."

Thomas and Stacey grabbed their containers and headed as close to the dome as they dared. They started the circle at the same point. Thomas started to move counter clockwise, while Stacey moved clockwise around the dome.

"See you on the other side." Stacey winked.

Thomas raised his eyebrows in acknowledgement and smirked.

It was awkward and cumbersome trying to carry the four containers and carefully pour the salt out. The ring had to be connected all the way around, and they didn't have the luxury of going back and forth to grab a new container when the old one ran out.

Thomas moved as quickly as he could. Knees bent, and hunched over slightly, Thomas shook salt out, forming the circle. As he shifted sideways, he looked back and forth from the circle to the dome, making sure to stay aware of what was going on inside.

The robed figures, who were standing in a semicircle, all now had a featureless entity attached to them.

Thomas had reached just past halfway of his side of the circle when the figure at the end closest to him noticed him. The entity and the human host turned their heads toward Thomas in unison.

Thomas froze for a moment.

The possessed started walking toward the back of the dome. The entity appeared to be puppeting the cultist, using the person as both a mount, and as an extension of its own limbs.

Thomas moved as quickly as he could. He could feel panic rising. It should be stuck inside the dome though. Unless…

"Shit."

At the other end of the dome was an open "employees only" door.

Thomas focused on getting to the end to complete the circle before the entity could get out the door.

"Come on, come on, come on!"

As he got closer to the door, he could see Stacey coming around on her end. She was slightly behind relative to where Thomas was in completion.

It was going to be close.

Thomas's heart was racing. He was almost even with the door frame.

The possessed cultist barreled through the open door and struck Thomas in the chest.

Thomas fell back. He somehow kept his grip on the remaining salt container, even as he, and the bottom of the container, hit the ground. A good amount of salt had splashed out of the container and onto the ground. Pain coursed through Thomas's back.

The possessed cultist stepped toward Thomas, who was still on the ground.

Thomas grabbed a handful of the spilled salt and chucked it at the cultist. Both the cultist and the entity flinched in pain.

Thomas attempted to scoot back and get up, but the possessed had recovered enough to grab Thomas around the throat and start to lift him up.

The possessed let out a howl. Smoke came from the cultist's forehead where a hand pressed a cross.

Maxwell drove the possessed back, forcing it to let go of Thomas.

Thomas stepped back, rubbed his throat, and tried to catch his breath. He watched as Maxwell pushed the puppeted cultist back into the dome.

Maxwell slammed the door shut and got out of the way as Stacey completed the circle of salt.

"Are you alright, Griff?" Stacey put her hand on Thomas's back in concern.

Thomas nodded and coughed.

"I owe you one, Doc."

"Don't mention it. Just glad we showed up when we did."

"I'm guessing Michelle figured out the right power levels then?"

Maxwell nodded. "She's getting things fired up as we speak."

The trio rushed over to the control room.

"Hey," Michelle greeted everyone. "Everything is ready to go. I have the settings programmed. All I have to do is click."

Thomas looked at everyone, making sure they were on board.

"Do it."

Michelle clicked go, and confirmed the new settings. The monitor displayed the change to the formation, which altered to the inverted image almost instantaneously.

"There we go!" Michelle was proud of her work. "So. How do we know it's working?"

They all looked at eachother.

"I'm just gonna have to go see." Thomas shrugged. "Not going to know otherwise."

"I'll join you," Stacey volunteered.

"Obviously, I have to monitor the settings here." Michelle had already had her fill of scary for the day.

"I'll stay here too." Maxwell seemed torn on what to do. "Make sure no one sneaks in from behind."

"Alright, team." Thomas nodded at everyone. "Let's do this."

Thomas retrieved the dropped salt container, and he and Stacey hurried around the dome to get back to the front. They saw the possessed that had attacked Thomas was trying to get out, but it appeared the mercury was doing its job.

They looked several times into the dome as they ran, but didn't get a full view until they stopped at the front.

The puppetted cultists still stood in a semi circle about the portal. They had been joined by two beings Thomas had discovered on the video. The two abominations stood at either side of the ovoid, their bodies constantly twitching. The faces in their flesh oozed some grotesque sludge around their bodies. The sickening, slug-like tendrils on their backs and shoulders quivered.

Within the light of the portal, something else had begun to appear. The head of this new being had to have been over six feet tall alone. Its face was birdlike, though a twisted mockery. The vile tendrils on its head squirmed. Two long, arm-like extremities came into view, the ends of which also had several of the tendrils extending from them.

Thomas tightened his grip on the container and stepped forward.

"Wait." Stacey grabbed Thomas's arm. "Look."

The monstrous abomination struggled to continue its attempt to emerge from the portal. An unearthly howl of frustration erupted from the creature. The arms retreated back into the void, and soon the horrible visage faded from view.

Beams of the blue light shot out from the ovoid, piercings through all the entities that had come through. They all, including their human hosts, began to dissolve, their astral particles swirling up the beams and back into the portal. Only the leader cultist, who had not been a host, remained.

The ovoid swelled. The blue turning an almost blazing white. The expansion stopped, then imploded. The force pulled the dome down around it.

Thomas instinctively put his arm up, and turned his body to shield Stacey.

The sound of the crashing dome had ceased, and Thomas and Stacey looked back at it.

The portal was gone. All that remained was the rubble of the destroyed dome, and the now destroyed landscaping that had been within.

***

"Turn right at the dirt road coming up, and that should take us to the Killarney House." Stacey double checked the GPS and pointed out the road to Thomas.

The months following the resort investigation had been a renewal in Thomas and Stacey's relationship. She had renegotiated her contract with the show to do primarily web calls for her research. After the experience at the resort, she and Thomas had new focus on their work.

Michelle and Maxwell, while not having quit their day jobs, had joined Thomas and Stacey's team.

They still did standard paranormal investigations, but prioritized any with possible connections to the realm they had all become familiar with.

DiAngelo was presumed missing. No body was found in the rubble, making it impossible to conclude with any certainty where he was.

Liability waivers, as well as the back up of what Langston referred to as the "cynical truth of money being the great comforter," ensured minimal backlash resulting from the two missing, presumed dead, employees that had apparently made up part of the cult group. The other people that had been present were unknown, presumably brought in by DiAngelo. The cultist that Alice and Thomas took down was going to be charged with trespassing and destruction of property, but was found dead by suicide in his cell.

The whole event was written off as an attempt to steal company secrets gone wrong. It was a simpler, and more believable story than the truth.

"And there she is," Stacey said, as the Killarney House came into view.

Thomas parked the van in front of the house.

The house curator walked outside through the front door and raised his hand in greeting.

Thomas looked at the team.

"Ya'll ready?"

Everyone nodded.

"Let's do this."

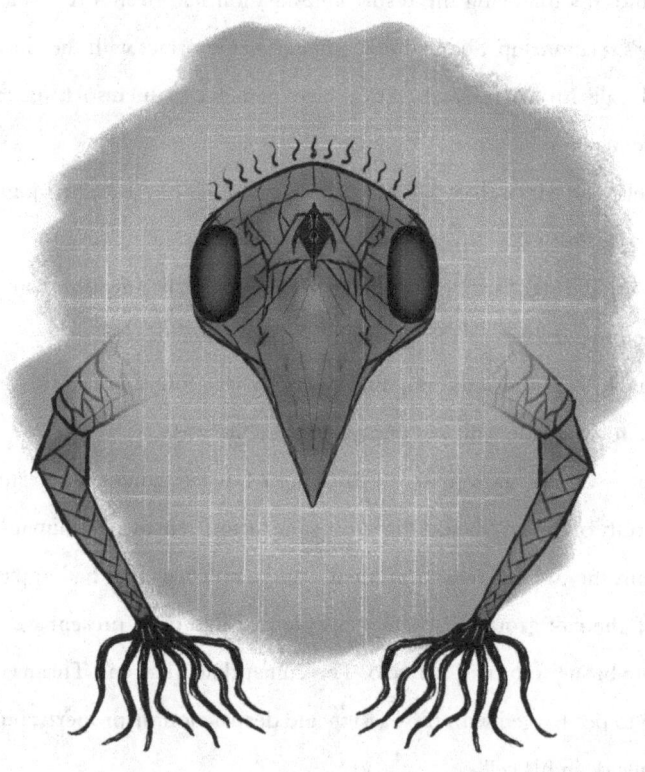

THE PRIMROSE WAY

Andrew returned from the funeral angry and distraught. It wasn't fair. An aneurysm had taken his wife. She died at the hospital. The doctors had failed him. God had failed him. And now, at 26, he was a widower.

There had to be a way to get her back. He had done some study of dark magics in the past. He knew portals could be opened. Deals could be made. If God hadn't listened to the desperate pleas he made that night in the hospital, then maybe someone, or something, else would listen to him now.

He had a few books which offered rituals and guidance on opening the borders and summoning lesser daemons, but he wanted something more powerful.

He spent the next day scouring every bookstore and curiosity shop he could find, buying every book he could get his hands on.

"These things can be dangerous," warned one bookseller upon seeing that Andrew had purchased every occult book in stock. Andrew's responding glare led the bookseller to shrug in a manner of "don't say I didn't warn you" and told Andrew what he owed.

Andrew read every page of every book. He didn't eat. He didn't sleep. His obsession grew with every word. Analyzing every ritual, every symbol, until, finally, he found the one. The goal of the ritual was to summon Satan himself, or at least someone like him. This ritual seemed to hold the most power, and the symbols filled Andrew with an excited dread.

He made sure he had the chalk and candles ready. The night of the new moon arrived soon, and Andrew was ready to summon who he needed.

On that night, he drew the circle. By sparse candlelight, Andrew meticulously copied every symbol within the ominous, twisted shapes he made appear in chalk on the floor of his garage. He wrote words in languages he did not understand. Every line was copied perfectly. He recreated the images from the book to such exactness, it was as if it had appeared from the page to the floor. He set up the ritual candles and lit them, their light barely penetrated the strange, heavy darkness that had set in. Andrew knelt facing south, and began to read from the book.

"I call upon the ancient powers, and to the one that was before. Open the gates between our worlds. From the four corners, I summon thee. From the four winds, I summon thee. From the four elements, I summon thee. Come forth now, and hear my request!"

Nothing.

"Come forth now!"

Andrew saw nothing but the flickering candles. He heard nothing but his own desperate breathing. He threw the book down and clasped his hands on the back of his head.

"Come forth now!"

His voice cracked, the petulant scream of a child not getting his way.

Andrew slammed his hands on the ground, got up, and stormed out of the door leading back into the house. In his anger, he did not notice the candles wavering and the shadow that rose up, nor when the candles went out of their own accord as he slammed the door behind him.

Hunched over in exhaustion and rage, Andrew slammed his fist back against the door. Once he had composed himself, he looked up and saw The Stranger sitting at the head of the kitchen table.

The Stranger was well dressed in dress shoes, slacks, a button down shirt, and a vest. He sat angled away from the table towards the door Andrew was leaning against in fear. The Stranger sat casually, leaning with his right elbow on the table, as looked at the time on his silver pocket watch which he held in his left hand.

"Sit down, Andrew."

The Stranger's voice had a deep resonance, as if pitched slightly lower than that of any human, and vibrated as if some faraway chorus of demons spoke with him.

The Stranger looked up from his pocket watch, looked away, and, finally, looked at Andrew, tracking his movements as he timidly approached the table and sat at the other end. The Stranger looked to his pocket watch again.

"Why have you called me here?"

"My— my wife. She was sick— the doctors. They couldn't do anything for her. And now. Now she's dead. I want her back."

The Stranger waited a moment before snapping his pocket watch shut. "No."

"What?" Exasperated and confused.

"I have fulfilled many men's desires. Satisfied their lust for power, for wealth, for sex. Allowed my lesser demons to fulfill various wishes. But despite what you may think, I am not some fucking genie." The Stranger's anger grew. "I do not exist to satisfy every whim that man may have. Your wife is dead. You ask me to undo what has already been done? It was her time. Be done with it and move on." The Stranger rose to leave.

"No! I won't accept that!" Andrew's tantrum raised the ire of The Stranger, who quickly spun around and strode toward Andrew.

Andrew shrunk back into his chair as The Stranger, though still several steps away, towered over him.

"I know I'm asking a lot." Andrew's tone returned to pleading timidity. "And I know there's a price to pay. But I'll do anything. Sell my soul. Whatever the price is, I'll pay it. I just. I just want more time."

The Stranger, who had returned to looking at the pocket watch, closed it and returned it to his pocket. "Very well. I'll bring your wife back to you. But this will be our arrangement. I will return at a time of my choosing to collect my payment. Is this agreeable?" The last word dripped with sarcasm.

"Yes."

"Then a bargain has been struck. A deal has been made!" The Strangers' voice grew louder, and filled the house like hellish thunder. "Let all who dwell above and dwell below bear witness to this, our pact."

The Stranger's right hand came down upon Andrew's left shoulder, now somehow behind where Andrew sat. Andrew's heart rate and breathing increased in fear as The Stranger leaned in.

"It is done." He emphasized each word as he spoke them in a gutteral whisper.

Andrew woke up with a start. He gasped and breathed in panic. His nightmare faded, but the fear lingered.

"Drew, are you up? Breakfast is ready."

His wife's voice pulled him out of the lingering dream fog.

"Yeah, yeah I'm awake! I'll be right there!" His wife always made incredible food, and Andrew had never grown tired of a good breakfast. He got out of bed, grabbing at his left shoulder as a sharp pain coursed through it. "Must have slept funny." Andrew rubbed his sore shoulder, shook off the rest of the remaining sleep, and headed to the kitchen for breakfast.

***

Over the next few years, what little memory of that night's events faded completely from Andrew's mind. There were strange dreams, and the occasional pain in his shoulder, but he ignored whatever subconscious warning they presented.

Life was good. The money that came along with the promotions they had received at their respective jobs would come in handy now that they were going to have their first child. Nine months passed, and their son was born. It was a happy time. In fact, Andrew couldn't remember a time that he had been happier.

He smiled as he looked at the decorations from his son's first birthday party. He would clean them up in the morning. It had been an exhausting, but joyous day.

Andrew had woken up and was getting a drink in the kitchen. He opened the fridge and, after drinking from the orange juice carton, put it back and closed the door.

Suddenly, The Stranger was there, leaning against the wall. The pocket watch closed, and The Stranger replaced it to his pocket. "It's time."

"No. No no. Please. I need. Please, I need more time."

The Stranger walked slowly and deliberately toward Andrew, annoyed at his constant pleading.

Andrew took a few steps backward, then stopped. His shoulders slumped, and he finally resigned himself to his fate.

"Fine." Andrew sighed. "You can have my soul."

The Stranger grinned and laughed mockingly. "Why would I want what's already mine?"

Confusion contorted Andrew's face as The Stranger reached out and grabbed Andrew's shoulder. Demonic screeching filled Andrew's ears as he felt his essence being pushed deep within himself. The Stranger took control.

Andrew, now visibly alone in the kitchen, reached his left hand down to his waist. His hand turned as if removing something from a pocket. Palm upward, Andrew's thumb moved as if depressing the crown of a pocket watch. He completed the pantomime by checking the time, closing the watch, and returning it to his pocket. He then turned, opened a kitchen drawer and removed a large knife. He twirled the knife in his hand as he walked to the bedroom.

"Drew?" His wife's groggy voice. "Drew. What are you doing? Andrew? Andrew? What are you doing?" Panic and fear. "Stop it, Andrew! Andrew! No!" Her screams filled the house as the knife plunged into her over and over. The baby's screams and cries soon joined in, awoken by his mother's screams. His cries were soon silenced just as his mother's were.

Andrew walked back into the kitchen. His shirt, hands, and the knife were soaked in the blood of his wife and son. He convulsed briefly before collapsing to his knees. The knife clattered on the floor of the kitchen, splashing blood on the tiles. Andrew looked at his hands and shirt. He realized the haze he had been in was no dream. The weight of the horror of what he had done fell heavy upon him. He raised his head and saw The Stranger standing above him. He closed the pocket watch one last time.

GAZEBeyondAR

The hype leading up to the release of GAZEbeyondAR was otherworldly. The mystery surrounding the game's development had attracted a lot more interest in the game than maybe it would have received otherwise. A brand new startup company releasing a horror game for mobile wasn't all that unusual. However, landing spots at all the major conferences, in addition to the extensive viral marketing— that was pretty unusual. There seemed to be money behind the game, but no one knew anything about the backers. The advertising seemed to be working, as GAZEbeyondAR was the most anticipated mobile game in history. Its pre-orders rivaled even some major studios' AAA titles.

The game was released on the morning of October 31st. Jason, like so many others, woke to find a new icon on his phone. The icon's symbol had star-like elements, but had hooked and curved lines cutting through and jutting out. The extra flourishes and markings gave it an ancient, mysterious feel. Jason appreciated that they had stayed away from simply slapping a pentagram on it and calling it a day. While the release date was a little too on-the-nose, the icon was well-executed and felt familiar, yet unique, and oddly "real," all at the same time.

There was a special, in-game event scheduled for halloween night to celebrate the release. Special one-time badges, items, and such, to celebrate the release. Again, great marketing, but Jason wondered if the servers could handle the activity. If as many people logged in as was anticipated, the game had a high chance of crashing. It had happened with other major releases, and it took months to work out the kinks. Jason, assuming this game lived up to the hype, didn't want to spend his entire evening trying to log in.

Jason decided to give the game a quick look as he got ready for work. He put in his headphones, since the game said that would lead to the best experience. He granted access to his phone's camera and microphone, and agreed to the terms of service.

Jason did a brief pass of the room as he walked to the bathroom. There were faint shimmerings in the image displayed on his phone. Without a tutorial, Jason wasn't totally sure what was going on, but it was an interesting, and slightly unnerving, effect.

Setting the phone on the bathroom counter, Jason finished getting ready for work. Suddenly, there was a scritch sound to his left. Jason froze for a second, then realized he heard it in his headphones. He picked up his phone, looked into the screen, and slowly turned toward the sound. As he turned, a ghoulish creature came into view. It was hunched over at the far end of the adjoining room, scratching the ground and sniffing the air. The gruesome thing appeared to have no eyes. The image appeared to actually sit on the ground, not float above it. The creature didn't look superimposed, as was the issue with many AR games.

As Jason held the phone fixed on the ghoul, various icons appeared on the right side of the screen, each filling up the longer he held the creature centered in the screen. Research appeared to be some part of the game, Jason thought to himself, though he was mostly impressed with the seamless integration of the generated image he focused on.

The shimmers he had initially seen were still present, though still faint. Jason found his gaze drawn to those images, like some instinct was pulling his thoughts toward them. Looking at the images was like trying to look through a twisted prism that is indistinguishable from air itself. Jason's focus returned to the ghoul. He was equal parts mesmerized by the grotesque design, and impressed by the advanced use of AR.

"This is pretty cool."

No sooner had Jason said the words out loud, the creature turned its head toward him and charged.

"Holy fuck!" Jason instinctively threw the bathroom door closed, nearly dropping his phone in shock.

He started laughing. That nervous laugh of relief and exhilaration. Jason closed the app. "That was good." Still laughing in admiration of the game's design and the use of jump scares.

At work, Jason's thoughts were consumed with the game. He had only played for a few minutes really, but there was this itch that he needed to scratch. He saw the occasional person pass by who appeared to be playing. Staring through their phones, occasionally startled, but mostly just transfixed on whatever they were looking at. Jason felt jealous. He wanted to see those shimmers again. He shook his head, surprised by his own fixation. He refocused on work, but still had an excitement for whatever Halloween night had in store for the game.

Evening came. Trick or treaters were out. The usual groups of younger children before sundown, and then more after. Standard mix of costumes, ranging from the traditional, to whatever was popular in film that year. There seemed to be a lot more people out this year. And certainly a lot more on their phones. As the younger children went home, and the sun began to set, more of the "older" crowd appeared. From 16 to early 40s, almost everyone had phones out and headphones in. Pace slow and deliberate. Not saying much, as they had seemed to learn that mechanic of the game. Jason stared into his phone, joining the crowds as the night grew darker. The event had begun. The shimmers, those dark prisms, appeared to solidify. More concrete, yet still so elusive. The more the people gazed, the more defined the shimmers became. Soon, strange, incomprehensible creatures emerged, as if birthed from the eldritch chrysalides, boring their way from a separate reality into the one of the gazers.

Jason felt fear like never before. He wanted to look away, but found his eyes transfixed on these horrors, and unable to switch off his phone.

Silence.

Silence was the key.

Don't make a sound and they won't know you are there.

That's how the game worked, right?

Jason's mind began to shatter as his fear gave way to undiluted terror.

The creatures were gazing back.

The other-planar aberrations slowly manifested in the air surrounding the crowds, visible now to the naked eye. They, ever so greedily, began to drink the life energy of their victims. Mind, body, and soul drained into these wicked things. As they had their fill, they savored the passing of the nectar from them into something beyond.

In the dark sky of Halloween night, when the borders between our world and all those that surround us are weakest, the moon was ever so steadily eclipsed by a growing shimmer.

INSOMNIBUS

I've always felt excitement and nervousness before a band goes on. The energy from the crowd. A subconscious worry the band will suck during a live performance. The anticipation of hearing and experiencing versions of songs that will only exist in that moment. The attitude and presence of the band itself. The shared experience that can never truly be captured or understood unless you were there.

My anxiety is always enhanced by my own dislike of crowds which, I suppose, stands in strong contention with my personal love of live music— one of the reasons I tend to stand on the outer edges of the crowd.

Tonight held more anticipation than usual. Insomnibus rarely toured, given the group had disbanded roughly twenty years ago, shortly after the release of their second album.. Those two albums, however, were highly influential in the genre, and the bassist, Cal, and guitarist, Mike, had gone on to front two other bands that were highly successful in their own right. They would occasionally get together to record and release a song or two under their original moniker, but it wasn't until last year that they finally released a new full album.

This alone, I felt, justified my excitement and agitation. I had an additional reason for being here, however, and it amped up my already nervous expectancy. My eyes darted around the crowd. I was suddenly filled with doubt and anxiety about being here.

My thoughts were as broken as an audio sample from some forgotten movie that was used on the new album played through the speakers. The rhythmic thud of the bass drum soon followed. The heavy distortion of the guitar filled in an in-time, but seemingly disjointed, riff. The bass started to add the same. Eight strikes down on the toms and all three instruments unified in a thunderous and mighty wave.

I allowed the music to sweep over me and let the visions it invoked become clear in my mind. As my body swayed, and my head nodded with the rhythm of the music, my consciousness began to slip into another time. I could see the ancient step pyramids that stood as monuments and places of worship for the ancient gods that once ruled this planet. High above the tops of the massive structures, winged beasts circled. Their gray flesh blotted with dark green patches, not unlike the moss and vine encased corners of the step pyramids. Hideous humanoid beings ungelated and worshiped at the bases. The grotesque half spawn of man and the twisted offspring servants of the god they called out to.

My vision pulled back, and I was again fully aware of my surroundings. I opened my eyes, which were now adjusted to the relative dark of the concert venue. I looked to my right, catching the eye of the attractive bartender, who smiled sweetly. If I hadn't had my current task at hand, and if I was a braver man, I would have spoken to her. Instead, I smiled softly back, sheepishly averted my gaze, and scanned the crowd.

I saw what I was looking for. There were only three, but there, interspersed among the concert goers, were the same spawn I had seen in my vision. The music was calling them up. I knew what I had to do.

The concert eventually ended, and I made my way outside. I walked to the side of the venue, hands in my pockets, head down, shoulders hunched, as it was lightly raining. I crossed the street, and turned down an alleyway that ran between two buildings across from the venue. I stood under what awning I could find, lit a cigarette, and waited. The smell from the dumpster, graciously, wasn't unbearable, and the smoke from the cigarette helped block that sweet and sick smell of rot. I wasn't sure how long I would need to wait, but I would wait as long as I needed to.

I sensed the presence of my quarry before I saw him. One of the people I had seen shapeshift into creature form during the concert was ambling across the street and turned down the alleyway between the concert venue and the building next door. I took one last drag of my cigarette before dropping it on the wet ground. The hiss was soon extinguished, as was the cigarette, after I put the ball of my foot to it.

Thankfully, the crowd had fully dispersed so no one watched me as I briskly walked across the street and followed the half-spawn into the alley.

I carefully, and quietly, began preparing a spell. I did not want to draw too much power too quickly. I also didn't want my target to become aware of the changes in energy before I was ready to deal with the creature on my terms. I was, admittedly, highly inexperienced in my current endeavor. My studies in magic, and the harnessing of said power, had been mostly theoretical, and certainly nothing to the extent at which I was about to enact. My thoughts quickly flooded with all the ways this could go sideways and how I was probably in over my head. Those thoughts were interrupted when I sensed some new and powerful energy.

At the end of the alley the half-spawn and I had been walking down, the band's guitarist appeared. Mike's tattoos glowed bright gold as he summoned energy. The half-spawn, now shifting between its human and creature form, turned around and ran. I reacted as quickly as I could, clumsily finishing the spell. A ball of sparking neon pink energy lept from my hands like the minor flames of a gas station firework. The creature lashed out with one of its flailing limbs, knocking me back as it ran past. I fell back, painfully falling on my ass, but gaining some comfort in seeing my spell had enough power behind it to slightly trip up the half-spawn.

I got up off the wet ground as Mike ran past, giving chase, huffing and puffing, clearly out of shape. The creature neared the entrance of the alley when Cal stepped out, blocking the exit. He waved his arms in front of him in a circular motion, summoning forth a large circular shield-like manifestation of deep purple energy. Cal pushed the shield forward, helping it meet the half spawn that ran at full speed. The impact knocked the creature flat on its back, which allowed Mike to catch up. The gold energy flowed fully into his hand, which he brought down onto the creature's chest. The half spawn glowed briefly before dissipating in a cloud of particles in a strange, silent poof.

Mike had his hands on his knees, still catching his breath. "What is it they always say in the movies? 'I'm getting too old for this shit?'" Mike pointed to himself. "I feel that. That's me."

Cal chuckled. He nodded and gestured toward me as I approached.

Mike turned around. "Thanks for the assist."

"Yeah. No problem. I mean, I don't know how much I helped, but, yeah."

"First time?"

I nodded.

"It gets easier. Sort of. I don't fuckin' know." Mike stood straight again and stretched his back.

"We should probably get out of here." Cal looked around, scanning for witnesses.

Mike nodded in agreement and motioned for me to follow them. We made our way to their tour bus, which Cal entered and Mike sat down on the step of the entrance. Mike lit a joint, took a toke, and handed it to me. Feeling it would be rude to refuse, I accepted, took a toke myself, then handed it back.

"Helps calm the nerves after all that. The energy you use takes a fuckin' toll after a while."

"How long you been...?" I gestured with my head back to the alley.

"Twenty-five years now? Long story short, we started seeing the reality of what was going on. Barriers between the worlds getting thin. Shit like that. Figured we'd do what we could to, I dunno, hold back the flood. Kind of feels like that whole Dutch kid sticking his fingers in the fucking dam or whatever, but..." Mike shrugged. "How'd you figure out we were doing this?"

"Had been delving into the occult and stuff like that. That led me to more mystical and ancient shit. Started to notice how yalls artwork, lyrics, rhythms, and everything were connected to the more bizarre things I was discovering. At the same time, I was becoming aware of the esoteric reality that exists around us. Helped me connect the dots. One and one and one is three kinda thing I guess."

Mike nodded. "What if you were wrong, and we were using all that for show?"

I shrugged. "Still got to enjoy a kickass show."

Mike laughed. "Good answer."

Cal appeared at the doorway of the tour bus. He tossed a book to me.

The book looked old, bound in some kind of leather, with strange runes on the cover.

"That helped us," Cal said. "Should help you too."

"Thanks," I responded, lifting the book in appreciation.

Cal nodded.

"Welp," Mike slowly stood. "The road calls. The next gig awaits." He handed the joint to me.

I tucked the book under my left arm, accepted the joint, and shook Mike's hand.

"Good luck out there."

"Yeah yeah! You too." I was still in shock.

Mike nodded. Cal gave a brief salute of acknowledgement. They both disappeared into the bus which started its journey to the next town.

I smoked the last of the joint as I watched the bus drive off into the night.

THE OLD MAN

I first noticed The Old Man in my youth. At least, that's when I think I did. My recollection of the exact time and date are a bit fuzzy, though I suppose it doesn't really matter. The point is, The Old Man was there.

It was the vauguest of recognitions, I suppose, but I could see him, even if just out of the corner of my eye. Some days closer than others. Even on days when I didn't see him, or think about him, I assume The Old Man was still there, watching, and grinning that unbreaking twisted grin of his.

If pressed, I would say my first true memory of The Old Man was when I was about seven. I got into a scuffle on the playground, as kids do. I was knocked down into the mulch by a kid my age, so I grabbed his ankle and tripped him, causing him to fall as well. That was the end of it. Well, not counting being scolded by various adults for my actions. Their words, however, were lost as my focus had turned to a figure standing some distance away. Watching. Grinning.

As I grew older, I tried to live my life as normally as I could. I pursued my interests to the best of my abilities— made friends and acquaintances. Though, in all honesty, these were cursory attempts. I never allowed my roots to grow deep, and I never allowed myself to truly pursue the things I wanted to pursue. My decision to hold back was mine alone, but the presence of The Old Man certainly influenced this.

The argument could be made, as I have even argued with myself, that I allowed The Old Man to have too much power and influence. I, of course, made every attempt to ignore him. To forget that he existed. Mercifully, I would, at times, genuinely forget that he was there. But I know my choices in life have always been rooted in the knowledge of The Old Man's presence.

What if he shows up?

What if people find out?

That second thought was the most prevailing. How could I explain The Old Man to others? How does one tell another, no matter how close you are to them, about a presence that dogs you no matter where you go? How could I explain the grotesque appearance? That he was always with me?

I knew, deep down, no one could ever understand. So I kept my secret and tried to live a normal life. Well, as normal of a life as he would allow.

I remember the first time I tried to kill The Old Man.

I had no idea what I was doing, or how to go about it, but I knew I had to try.

It was a simple attempt, but at least I had built the resolve to try. I had never confronted The Old Man before in any way, so perhaps my first attempt seems a touch extreme. But, if you knew The Old Man, as I do, you would also know words would have been fruitless. I chose to challenge The Old Man with violence. My hands gripped the bat tightly. I shook with nervousness. To finally face this thing that had haunted me my entire life. I swung, connecting with The Old Man's head. To feel his skull give way, and to hear that crunch of wood on bone was glorious. To see the scattering of teeth like confetti at a celebration. I have never felt such exaltation before, or since.

He fell.

I was free.

I felt a renewed confidence. It was like I could see the world more clearly with him gone.

But a week later he was back. I could see The Old Man standing there.

Staring.

Grinning.

I felt the new life I thought I had found crumble around me. Disheartened and crushed, I fell into an isolation which surpassed any I had embraced before.

I made several more attempts at killing The Old Man, with the same results.

This last time, I took a rock and crushed his rotted grin. I struck over, and over, and over. His face caved in. Feeling, and seeing, and hearing his fetid bones crunch and splatter. I felt no joyful release. Only desperation. I put the bastard down. Buried him face down in the dirt, and covered his corpse with stones.

I moved away.

I changed my name.

But The Old Man is through the gate again, banging on my door. He's shambled back from where I left his corpse.

I have no one to turn to. No one that would understand.

I lie here, curled up like that will protect me. I keep no light on. My stomach is hollow. As is my heart. My throat aches, and my mouth hangs open, but I do not weep. Waves of cold course through me from within. How can I defeat that which will not die? The Old Man will find his way inside soon enough. I fear I have no other recourse to stand against him and I lack the strength to carry on.

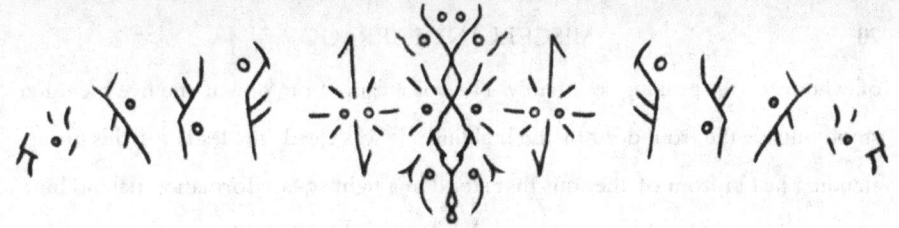

SOJOURN

I woke up in a clean and brightly-lit attic. There was nothing stored here. Completely empty, save for my slowly rising body as I pushed myself up to a seated position. I shook off whatever lingering disorientation was left in an attempt to get my bearings.

The attic was made of a light colored wood. Floor. Walls. Ceiling. All cedar, and not uncomfortable to lay on. I'm not sure why I was so certain it was cedar. I was no craftsman or woodworker.

Was I?

No. Definitely not.

Name?

Nothing.

How did I get here?

An even deeper mystery.

A single window in the middle of the wall I was currently seated against allowed sunlight to spill into the room. I was surprised it wasn't sweltering, given I could see no ventilation and the room was bathed in sunlight. To the contrary, I was quite comfortable.

I wore some kind of generic running shoes, jeans, belt, and a dark green t-shirt. Not my style, but I was certainly in no position to be choosey. I suppose things could be much worse.. I could have been naked in some dank, dingy cellar. It's funny how perspective makes you appreciate the tiniest of blessings.

My attention was soon drawn to the sound of voices outside. The words were indistinguishable, but I could tell by the cadence of the sounds that it was speech.

Curious, I ever-so-carefully peeked outside, hoping to at least catch a glimpse of whoever was speaking so intently. The voice came from one of the five men that stood outside the front door of the building. He was clearly the leader of this group, standing just in front of the four that stood in a tight square formation behind him. They stood in the road, as there seemed to be no sidewalk, as the leader appeared to be arguing with whoever stood inside the building. His gestures and face displayed an emphatic ernestnestness, just short of anger. Their uniforms were predominantly black, with some silver and red trimming and accents. The leader's uniform was slightly different, with a jacket and captain's hat, which he held under his arm. The uniforms were not unlike a gestapo outfit, with modern design. It reminded me of something I might see in one the sci-fi films I was so fond of.

Why would I remember that?

The conversation appeared to end, as the leader donned his hat and the group turned to their left and headed down the street.

I dropped down quickly and, if I'm being honest, quite awkwardly, to ensure I wouldn't be seen.

I lay on my back, looking up at the ceiling for a moment, when the attic door, so seamlessly inscribed in the floor I had not noticed it before, opened.

"You can come down now." The voice that informed me was matter of fact, but not unfriendly.

I descended the wooden ladder placed at the opening and found myself in a clock and curio shop.

The shop was as clean and well lit as the attic, and, as strange as it was, I found it somewhat comforting to be surrounded by such pristine, though antique, pieces.

The shop's proprietor, and my apparent protector, was an older gentleman, perhaps in his late-sixties-early-seventies. Though, given the nature and condition of the items in the shop, I would not have been surprised if I had discovered he was much, much older.

Before I could speak, the old man waved his hand to stop me, a kind, half smile on his face.

"I know you have a multitude of questions, so I will tell everything I can, and everything I know. I have no idea how you got to this land, but you are not the first to come here. I have kept you safe as long as I can, but you must continue on your own now. There are others who will help you along the way. There is a safehouse somewhere to the west and north of this town, though I know not exactly where. They will know more about how you might get back home. Look for the bright and lazy eyes. There are others like you. You'll know them when you see them. If those men," he gestured toward the road, "or others in their... society... or whatever they are calling themselves these days, find you, your chances of getting back home will be effectively nil. And that way is north." He gestured straight ahead to the door of the shop. "I wish there was more I could do." There was deep sincerity in his words. "Good luck out there."

I nodded in appreciation, opened the door of the shop and, with a quick look to my right to make sure those men were not in sight, quickly made my exit and headed west down the road.

***

The initial part of my journey led me past, and through, small towns and hamlets, similar to the one I had started in. They had a western European architectural influence, like something on a postcard.

I kept my interactions with the citizens to less than a minimum, though I never got the feeling that any of them were out to get me, or were going to run to the authorities and report me. They seemed intentionally indifferent. My outfit certainly made me stand out from the regular citizenry, and it became clear I wasn't the first of whatever I was to have passed through.

I traded quick errands for a piece of fruit, or a small amount of currency, with those that were willing. I was sure to not stay long in any one place however, making sure to be gone within the hour. I slept hidden off the roads as best as I thought I could, among trees and hills.

Eventually, the landscape and sky changed. Overcast and gray, though still beautiful in its own way. I trudged along the much flatter planes of this new country I was in, finally seeing a town on the horizon.

It was larger than the ones I had passed through in the early part of my journey, and I soon saw it was of medieval architecture. The town square was busy, with vendor stalls and carts lining the streets and main square. Townsfolk were dressed as one would expect in a medieval town. They scurried to and fro, purchasing items at the stalls, while others seemed to prepare for an event.

Feeling hunger, certainly enhanced by the sights and smells of so many food vendors, I approached one of the fruit stalls. I pointed to an apple, then held out a coin that I had earned in one of the previous towns. I shrugged and made a face expressing my uncertainty if she would accept the currency from such a different land. She looked at the coin and then me, weighing her decision. She eventually relented, and accepted my trade. I nodded graciously, and with a "Thank you. Thank you." I picked up an apple, and made my way further into the town.

I took in the sights of the town as I savored the apple, walking around the square with the intent of heading back to the entrance of the town and getting on my way.

"The Fool! The Fool! The festival has found its fool!"

I had made it about three quarters around the square when I heard someone shouting. I looked about, and saw a man pointing at me and shouting.

"The Fool! The Fool!"

A cheer went up from the crowd.

My instinct to run kicked in, but many hands grabbed me before I could try to make an escape. I felt panic as I struggled against the group that had grabbed me, and more than a little pissed that I hadn't finished my apple that was now being kicked along the dirty ground by the shuffling feet of the people forcing me toward the stocks.

The heavy wooden bar was lowered over my neck and wrists, then locked, keeping me in a quite uncomfortable kneeling position. The stocks were on a slightly elevated platform in the middle of the town square, so the shouting crowd could all have a good look at me.

"The Fool! The Fool!"

The shouting was like a bizarre call and response chorus.

Then, something exploded right beside my head. A tomato, most likely, based on the smell and splattered wet that streaked across my face like some moist, chunky shrapnel.

That broke the seal, and I was bombarded with various fruits and vegetables. I suppose this was some form of release for the town during their festival. Relatively harmless in a sense, though incredibly embarrassing for the recipient. Which is the point. Though I will say, a cabbage to the face is quite painful.

I'm not sure how long the main barrage of vegetable matter lasted. It did die down eventually, with a few straggling jeers and produce thrown at me. Once evening came, the townsfolk left, and I remained in the stocks, exhausted and in pain. The chill of the night air wasn't necessarily a reprieve, but it was, at the very least, a variance in sensations. I closed my eyes and tried to focus on feeling the air, instead of the pain that was coursing through my body. Sleep was not going to happen, so this was the best I could do.

The sound of hooves and wooden wheels drew my attention away from my attempt at meditation. A cart came to a stop at the edge of the town square. The driver, at the instruction of the woman who sat next to him, stepped down from the cart and made his way over to the stocks.

The Lady sat regally, wearing a dark blue cloak, the neck lined with fur to keep out the cold. The moonlight reflected off her silver pendant. She quickly glanced my way before re-steadying her gaze. I vaguely recalled seeing her earlier that day, but I wasn't sure.

The driver released the lock, lifted the stock, and helped me to my feet. We made our way back to the cart, the driver mostly supporting me, my arm draped over his shoulder. He helped me into the back of the cart, and soon we were on our way.

My hand instinctively checked my face, which, like my ego, was bruised. I was in pain, but I would live.

The Lady and her driver took me some distance out of the town. I had dozed off, so I was not sure how far we traveled, but it was far enough that I couldn't see the town anymore.

The cart came to a stop, and I eased myself down and out of the back of the cart. I thanked the Lady, who gave a kind smile and a nod.

"North?"

She indicated the direction and I thanked her again.

The cart turned around and headed back to that strange town as I slowly made my way into the night.

***

I had walked for several days when I came upon a modern, suburban neighborhood. While this was the most familiar to me, it also, initially, seemed the most unusual, given the places I had passed through before. Though, in reality, nothing should have surprised me given the nature of the world in which I had been traveling.

The neighborhood was exactly as one would expect, I suppose. Sidewalks. Well-kept lawns. Children playing as the sun was just starting to set. Parents calling children to come in for dinner.

"Sir. Sir!"

One couple was standing just outside their front door as their three children jogged up from the lawn and into the house.

The mother tousled the hair of one of the kids as they ran past. The father continued to speak.

"Sir. You must join us for dinner. I can tell you've been walking far."

"That's ok. I really shouldn't."

"Please. We insist."

"We always have plenty of food. It's no bother." The mother added.

Their voices and body language seemed friendly enough, and I was hungry and tired. I quickly relented. "Okay. All right."

"Fantastic!" the mother said excitedly, as she turned to enter their house. "Children, set an extra place. We have a guest!"

"Well! Come in! Come in!" The father waved me in and I entered the home. "Please, have a seat." He gestured to the maroon couch in the living room.

"I mean, is there anything I can…"

He cut me off with a wave of his hand. "You're our guest. Just relax, and we will get everything ready."

I nodded and sat down.

He went to join his wife in the kitchen.

The maroon colored couch on which I sat was flush against the wall, and under the windows that faced the front yard. I looked at the eggshell-colored walls and beige carpet. The only decorations were two small vases that contained a few stalks of wheat and reeds. These vases stood on the mantle above the unlit fireplace. A low coffee table and a small chest filled out the rest of the room. Everything was clean, neat, and organized. So much so I began to grow uncomfortable.

My thoughts were interrupted when the youngest child showed me drawings she had made and a few of her favorite toys. She seemed genuine in her excitement to show me these things, and I, hopefully, put my growing unease aside enough to show proper interest back.

Dinner was soon announced, and the children ran to their seats.

Everyone was seated when I arrived at the dining room. I moved around to the empty chair at the place setting for the guest. There was no conversation. It was an odd silence that contrasted the earlier sounds of the preparation and the children moving about.

The mother smiled and gestured to the empty seat.

The youngest, who was seated across from the guest's seat, looked at me. A twinge of concern flashed across her face, and her eyes darted up.

I shook my head slightly, confused by the change in her demeanor. I pulled the chair back.

Her eyes darted up again. Her focus quickly alternated from me, to something high above.

I looked up.

I didn't see anything at first, but phasing into my vision was a dark, gelatinous mass attached to the vaulted ceiling directly above the guest seat. The vile ooze waited to feed—to envelop and chew with its many unseen, internal mouths.

"So what?" I kept my gaze on the disgusting mass on the ceiling. "I sit, eat, and in the middle of dinner that thing devours me?"

"You. You can see it?" The father spoke with surprise and remorse in his voice.

"We're sorry. We're so sorry." The mother's voice cracked with oncoming sorrow. "If we don't feed it," she continued, "it said it will hurt us. Hurt our children."

"What else could we do?" the father continued. "We were afraid. We made a deal that would keep us safe. Travelers come through often enough…" He hung his head. "I'm sorry."

To my surprise, I felt a great sadness within the core of my being, and not the anger I thought would overtake me. I was overcome with sorrow and sympathy for these people. These parents. They had done a great evil, to be sure, and I had no idea how many had been offered to that thing, nor did I wish to dwell on the thought. However, this could be their moment of redemption and I had no wish to further condemn them.

"You have to fight it." I watched the mass quiver, fold, and slop in and out of itself. "This is your home." I looked at the parents. "Take it back."

The father and mother nodded in newfound resolve. The youngest daughter smiled at me. I nodded, returning her smile with a sad, but hopeful, one of my own, then made my way back onto the street.

I wandered from neighborhood to neighborhood. I walked miles through all too similarly designed communities. I began to feel I was going nowhere. I felt lost in this suburban wasteland. Maybe I should have just let that thing eat and digest me however many nights ago that was. I told myself to stop thinking that way and to push on. I willed my legs to move and continued.

I walked another two blocks, and followed the road as it hooked right.

I saw it.

Bright and lazy eyes

A two story house. Two offset windows on the second story. Electric candles illuminated each.

"Please. Please be it." I offered a desperate prayer.

I approached the front door and knocked.

A very pretty brunette answered the door. "Quickly! Quickly!" She ushered me inside. "Father! Another one is here!"

Her father came down stairs. "Ah! Welcome, traveler. You are safe here. I will show you where you can rest."

He led me upstairs to a room where another man was sitting. He was black, around the same age as me, and wearing the same outfit as me, though his shirt was blue.

"Please, sit. Rest. We will bring you food, and we can discuss what your next steps are." The man left, leaving me and the other traveler alone in the room.

The other traveler greeted me. "Simon."

"Nice to meet you." I shook Simon's hand. "I, uh, don't remember my name."

He shrugged understandingly "My name is about the only thing I do remember before waking up in whatever bizarro world we are in."

"How'd you find your way here?" I asked.

"Let's see. Woke up in a barn in a haunted mountain hamlet. Went from there to some bombed out, post apocalyptic city. Then some hedge maze, garden, forest thing. All the while avoiding some gestapo looking guys. Some people helped me, and told me about this place, so here I am. You?"

"European town, medieval market, and suburban nightmare. At least that's what I can remember." I shrugged.

"Any idea how we got here?"

"Was hoping you could answer that."

Simon laughed. "I know we don't belong here. And it's like I know things, points of reference and stuff like that, that aren't part of this world. But I can't place where or why."

I nodded. "Same here. And, not to be weird, I feel like I know you for some reason."

"You know, I was about to say the same thing. It's weird. Not the weirdest thing I've experienced in this place, but still odd."

Our hosts came back up and brought us down for a meal.

The safehouse keeper and his daughter did not give us their names. They felt it was safer in case the worst happened.

"We don't want them stopping us from helping travelers like you," the daughter explained.

"Who are they, exactly?" asked Simon.

The Keeper shook his head. "Not sure. The Hunters, as some call them, have been around as far back as anyone can remember. They somehow know when a traveler arrives, and hunt them down. If they catch a traveler, they take them to the fortified city the Hunters control, and, well, no one knows what they do to them."

"Guess it's best to not find out," Simon said.

"Precisely." The Keeper nodded.

"So how do we get back to wherever we came from?" I asked.

"There is a portal," the Keeper replied. "It is at the end of the inside of a large brick. The brick sits in a field. They will be patrolling, so be careful."

Another mystery, but it was a step forward, and we felt like we were close to the end.

The next morning, we left at sunrise and began our journey to The Fields. We had a renewed vigor and hope that pushed us forward.

The neighborhood disappeared from view behind us. After a mercifully un-eventful half a day's walk we arrived at The Fields.

The Fields were broken up with wooden post and rail fences, some with barbed wire. Roads of clay also ran around the perimeter of several. The gestapo-like soldiers seemed to be everywhere.

Simon and I kept low and moved as quickly and quietly as we could. Holding our breath, we waited in a shallow ditch for a patrol to pass. My heart pounded in fear as we scurried across the clay road to the other side. Moving. Hiding. Ducking. Then we saw it.

An out of place office building tucked into the corner of one of the fields. Small and rectangular, from a distance it looked like one of the dark brown bricks from which it was made.

There were no patrols currently in sight, so we ran. We ran as fast as our tired legs would take us. We could see the door on the far left of the wall facing us. The entrance door was mercifully unlocked, saving us from having to break the tinted glass. I pulled the door open, and we stepped inside. There was only one way to go. We turned right and ran down the short hallway. The fourth and final door on the left. That had to be it. I reached the door first and pulled it open.

A dark void filled the space beyond the door frame. This was it. Passing through would take us home.

I turned and looked at Simon. He was standing about a meter away from me in the middle of the hallway.

"I can't go."

"What do you mean, Simon? It's right here!" I gestured to the doorway.

"No. I mean. I can't go." He raised his hand, balled it up, and struck an invisible wall with the side of his fist.

Confused, I stepped forward and reached out. My hand reached through as if nothing were there at all. "Give me your arm." I attempted to pull Simon through, but he simply struck against the barrier.

"Just go. It'll be alright," Simon said.

I hesitated.

"It's okay, man. I won't let those goons get me, but they might get us both if you don't get out of here."

I nodded, ramping myself up to jump into the void. "I'll come back. I'll figure out a way to get you out of here. I promise!"

I leapt into the doorway.

I had expected to fall, but instead I felt as if I was gliding forward. My orientation had not changed, yet I had the distinct sensation that I was headed up toward something. My breathing intensified as I could feel my destination growing closer. It felt like I was under water, but rushing to the surface. I instinctively closed my eyes.

My eyes opened, but I couldn't see much because of the blinding light. A rhythmic beeping was all I could hear beyond my own panicked breathing. Something was in my mouth and throat. I panicked, and painfully pulled some kind of tube out, feeling it scratch my throat. The overpowering smells of bleach, phenyl, and antiseptic filled my nose. I quickly pulled off various electrodes, and pulled out an IV. My anxious attempt to get out of the bed I was in resulted in me falling hard to the floor. Cold tile met my skin. My legs did not seem to want to work. I propelled myself forward in the weakest of crawls. I looked up. My vision had begun to clear. I could see a nurse rush toward me. Beyond her, I could see Simon in a hospital bed. A nurse wheeled away equipment to give Simon's parents and sister space to mourn. They had taken Simon off life support.

The nurse helped me up off the floor, ignoring my feeble attempts at struggle, and my hoarse, barely audible cries of "No! No!"

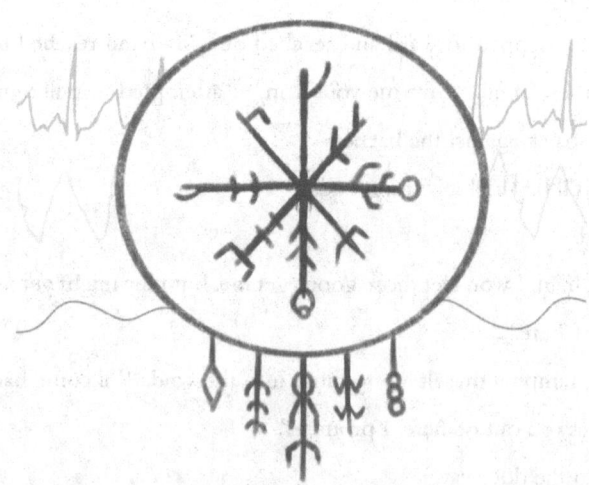

IMPERIUM

He stared at the materials in front of him. Pens. Pencils. Sketchbook. He picked up the book he had been reading and then promptly put it down. One hand absentmindedly played with his beard, while the other rotated the book to align with the rest of the clutter on the table. Sure, there were probably too many things out, but it was organized in a chaotic sort of way. He felt a metaphoric resonance in the clutter— trying to make some kind of sensible arrangement of the current mess. Or something like that.

He picked up a pencil and drew a few lines on a blank page in his sketchbook. The same few lines he tended to draw when there wasn't any inspiration or creativity ready to spring forth. Better than just staring at the blank page, he thought.

He took a sip of his coffee, just shy of cold at this point, and adjusted the volume on his headphones.

Then Melody walked up.

She looked like a Melody. Not in some stupid, sentimental way. Just that her name fit her look and presence. Like how some people look like a Scott, even though their real name might be Fred, or Julian. His mind raced with stupid thoughts like that. He always got nervous when she came around. He did his best to hide it.

"Hey," she said.

"Hey," he replied. He took his headphones out and paused the music.

"Can I sit for a minute?"

"Of course." His hands shook just enough to knock a few of the pens off the table as he moved his backpack to the floor and inched the clutter back. A bit of coffee splashed up and out when he moved the cup. He leaned down to pick up the pens that had fallen. He felt his cheeks get warm and flush. He closed his eyes tightly for a moment and clenched his teeth. *Fucking idiot.* He sat up, put the pens back on the table and managed a smile. "What's up?"

He'd had a crush on her for the two years he'd known her. His feelings had never seemed to lessen, despite how much time had passed. Sure, they would talk when they ran into each other, but usually it was a brief conversation. And she had never sat down with him before.

He placed a hand above his knee to stop his leg from bouncing.

"I..." Mel scrunched her nose and pursed her lips to one side. "I wanted to ask you something. It's probably... no it's gonna sound weird. But I know you are definitely someone who's interested in weird stuff." Her voice took a slightly higher pitch, to ensure that her statement didn't seem like an insult.

He let out a light chuckle. An understanding smirk appeared on his face. She wasn't wrong. He had been interested in the weird, the strange, and the unexplained from when he was very young. Not an expert by any means, but he probably knew a little more than most. His ability to engage in normal behavior and conversation probably helped with being approachable on those subjects. Stereotypes exist for a reason, so he was glad he didn't fall on the completely anti-social side of things. Close though. Regardless, it wasn't that odd that someone would want to ask him about something strange or "weird," but it was a little surprising that it was Mel. She had never struck him as the type to be interested in anything of that nature.

He noticed Mel repeatedly tugged at and rolled her left index finger between her right finger and thumb. Her eyes darted around, and she didn't make much eye contact. Her shoulders were up and in, and the muscles in her neck were taut. She had always greeted him with warmth and a smile— he never got the sense of anything but confidence in her voice. Something was definitely off.

She continued. "Have you listened to that *Imperium* podcast?"

"I have, actually."

"What did you think of it?" Mel tugged at her finger.

"I mean," he leaned back and scratched at his beard, "I listened to the whole first season. Binged it in a few days actually." He shrugged. "It was okay. The concept of

taking real mysterious disappearances and horrific murders and attempting to connect them into some greater narrative was kind of interesting. It's a creative way to
discuss those things, instead of just reading a wiki outloud. Jumping from mysteries
like Roanoke, Hoer Verde, and Ambrose Bierce, to Elisa Lam, to stuff like Howard
Unruh, Zodiac, and The Phantom Killer, and all that, was a little much, and maybe
in bad taste, but I get the concept. Taking all of that real world mystery and horror,
and using it for their own grand story of mystical and interdimensional connection
is a neat idea. The mysterious book that led him to make the connections, and the
interdimensional house thing was kinda cool too, I guess. Not necessarily original,
but I see what they were trying to do. But, I dunno, there was stuff I definitely didn't
like."

"Like what?" She chewed on her lower lip.

He shrugged. "I don't like the unnatural way people tend to talk on podcasts
in general, and *Imperium* had that issue. The voice acting in general was pretty weak.
The sound editing was off. The dialogue wasn't that well written. Sloppy storytelling.
That overly dramatic sound after every 'big discovery.'" He made air quotes. "Stuff
like that. Just felt amateurish from a performance and technical standpoint, I guess."

Mel let out a long sigh. Her shoulders lowered and she briefly closed her eyes.
Mel finally made eye contact, stopped fidgeting with her finger, and gave a soft smile.
"Thank God."

He cocked his head and scrunched his face. He shook his head slightly. "I'm,"
he dragged the word out. "I'm not sure what's going on?"

She laughed a little. "You're pretty much the first person I've talked to who's
listened to it that isn't, I dunno, psycho into it."

He chuckled.

"I listened to it too," she continued, "since so many people seemed to be really
into it, recommending it, and all that. I feel the same way as you. Just didn't do it for
me. Whenever I say that though, or criticize it in any way, people get almost hysteri-
cally enraged. Best way I can put it."

"Hmm." He crossed his arms and leaned back. "I had an experience like that too. I said the same things I just told you, was probably less harsh on the criticisms actually, and the person I was talking to got super pissed at me. Like I was insulting his personal dream project or something. It was weird."

"Right?!"

"But, I mean, I dunno, isn't that any fandom though?" He leaned forward, rested his forearms on his thighs, and folded his hands in front of him. "You say anything slightly negative, or don't sing the praises of whatever it is they are currently worshipping, and they lose their minds."

"Yeah. That's true. But you don't think it's, well, it's more than that?" Mel waved her hand, palm up. "It feels like more than just an overreaction. There's a real sense of anger and, well, hate from the people I know in that fandom."

He leaned back again. His right hand rubbed and scratched the back of his head as he thought for a moment. "I mean, based on my own experience, you're not wrong." He paused. "Can I ask why you're coming to me though?" He didn't mind that Mel was talking to him. Not in the least. Hell, he was happy to just get a smile, or a wave, or, especially, a "hi" from her.

"Like I mentioned before, I know you're into all the ghosts and aliens and paranormal stuff. You know. The 'weird' stuff.'"

"Oh. So I'm the 'weird guy' to you. Thanks." He put his hands up, shook his head, then smirked.

Mel laughed. "Not in a bad way." She smiled.

He chuckled, rubbed the back of his head again, then quickly gave a tug at his right ear, which he could feel growing hot. "Look," he sighed. "I don't know if something is going on, or if it's just people being people, but I'll do some digging and see what I can turn up. Don't know if that's what you wanted, but, hey, it'll at least give me something interesting to do." He gave his smirk smile.

Melody sighed and smiled again. "I know it could be nothing, but, yeah. That would be awesome."

"Hey, umm." Risk time. "Can I," he scratched the back of his head, "get your number so I can let you know as soon as I get some info together. Probably better than using social media."

"Oh, yeah. Of course."

They exchanged numbers and Melody got her things together to leave. "I'm so sorry, I've got to run."

"No worries." He shook his head.

Mel hesitated slightly, then gave him a quick hug. "Thank you."

"Of course." There was a slight surprise in his voice. Melody had never hugged him before.

"Just let me know what you find."

"I will." He gave a comforting smile.

"Bye." Her voice almost a whisper.

"Bye." His voice the same.

He watched Mel leave then turned back to the table. He put both elbows on the scratched wooden surface, leaned forward, scratched the sides of his head, then slid his palms over his eyes.

"Shit," he mumbled under his breath. He had some research to do.

***

A week later, he found himself walking up to the coffee shop. He chewed at his lower lip. He took deep breaths in through his nose and exhaled heavily through pursed lips. *Get it together.* He wasn't sure about what he had found or what any of it meant. But it did give him a chance to see Melody again, and he was happy about that. At the same time, he questioned his own reasons for helping her. Was it just about helping someone? The thrill of the mystery? Or was he just using her concern with the podcast as an opportunity to spend time with her? Probably thinking too much on it, especially since she had been the one to text him about meeting in person.

Found some info on what you were looking for.

Great! What's your schedule so you can show me :)

They had arranged a day and time to meet, although he could have just as easily text her his findings. He hadn't been keen on that idea, despite not being sure there was really anything going on. Leaving a trail might not be the best idea, and he wanted to take a better-safe-than-sorry approach. Mel might be thinking the same thing, given her request.

There was something about what he found that was eating at him, though he couldn't quite pin it down.

As he continued to approach the shop, his eyes darted around, as they usually did, taking a break from staring at the ground. When he did, he saw a woman sitting on the bench staring at him. He gave a quick half smile and then looked back at his feet. It felt like she was still staring. He kept his stride, pulled open the door to the coffee shop, and walked inside. It felt like every other person in there was watching him. They hadn't stopped what they were doing, just simply looked up. No emotion. More like observation. This wasn't the first time he had felt like people were oddly staring at him. His anxiety, among other things, led him to have this impression before, but that had always been a handful of people. This was much more than that. At least that's how it seemed. He tried to chalk it up to his own paranoia, but he still wasn't comfortable.

He scanned the shop for Mel and, upon seeing she had not arrived yet, got his coffee, and went to find a table outside. The weather was a bit cooler than normal for this time of year, which he enjoyed. He sent a text.

Sitting outside

Be there in 5 :)

He set his phone down and took a deep breath. He closed his eyes and slowly exhaled. A bit more calm came to him, but still… there was something.

"Hey! Sorry I'm late." Melody sat down at the connecting side of the square table to where he sat. "Been running around all day, so I'm a bit of a mess." Jeans, T-shirt, canvas shoes, messy bun, glasses.

You still look amazing, he thought.

Melody set her bag down. "You smell nice!"

He had forgotten he had applied beard oil before he left his house. He had also put on a button down shirt over his usual t-shirt and jeans look. "Thanks." *I'm an idiot.*

Mel smiled. "So whatcha got?"

He took a deep sigh to ready himself. "Alright. So. I'll go through this in some kind of order to try and make some sense of it. So..." He opened and unlocked his tablet, and opened up a composition book. He actually prefered paper and pen for writing and such. Not that he was against technology growth. He loved all the instant access he could have to music and research and movies, etc. He just liked, and missed, the tactile nature of things.

"...I started by looking at comments and reviews on the podcast's page on iTunes. A lot of it's generic 'OMG this is the greatest ever' nonsense. But..." he scrolled down the reviews, "...there is a review basically saying the same things we were saying about it. Voice acting. Sound production. Blah blah blah. And here. Read the review that is responding to that one." He turned the screen so she could see it.

"Okay. Let's see. 'I hope your body gets riddled with cancer and you suffer as you die.'" She paused. "'Umm 'Fuck you. I would kill you myself if you could.' Charming. Oh. And five stars." Mel's eyes widened, she shook her head in disbelief, and turned the tablet back.

"Yeah. It's the same on Reddit. A mix of generic discussion, people saying how it's the greatest thing ever, and super hostile responses to any negative critique." He paused to pull up the next piece on the web browser. "Okay. So I also found the podcast company's website."

Mel shifted closer, her left shoulder now touching his right. He tensed and gripped the seat of his chair with his left hand, about to scoot away. He released his hand instead, and gave the tablet a slight adjustment to make it easier for them to look at it together. "Read it," he finally continued, "and tell me if anything jumps out at you." His eyes darted back and forth a few times between the screen and Melody's profile as she read the webpage. He tried to make sure his eyes didn't linger.

"So that's fake, right?" Melody turned her head to look directly at him. "I mean, it feels like a made up history to go with their stories. 'Terrestrial Radio'? Who talks like that?"

"Hipster assholes?" he offered in reply.

Melody laughed.

He continued. "They are based out of the Pacific Northwest. Kind of ground zero for that stuff. But yeah, I agree. I'm pretty sure it's made up to make it sound like they were doing radio shows before this, but I couldn't find any evidence of that."

"That's weird though. Right?" Melody's lower lip ever so slightly protruded in a pout. There was a hint of disappointment in Melody's voice as she asked the question. He couldn't blame her. While a mundane answer might be the most plausible, it certainly wasn't the most interesting. Or exciting.

"If I'm playing rational skeptic," he over enunciated the last two words to not stumble over them, "then I'd have to say no, and just chalk it up to their terrible, pretentious writing. But," he added with emphasis, and raised a finger to stave Mel's possibly growing disappointment, "I did discover something I thought was very interesting." He started to pull up the next piece of information. "And what made it even more interesting was that I couldn't find anyone talking about this particular thing on any of the reddits or discussion boards." He pointed at the screen. "That is the actual LLC name of the company that, produces I guess, the podcasts."

"Emdosius, LLC?" Melody shook her head, nose scrunched in confusion.

"So," he had folded his hands, elbows on the table. He rested his head against the back of his hand and looked at Mel, "I'm not totally sure, and I could be reaching here, but I think it's supposed to be a play on the name Amdusias."

Melody shook her head again and chuckled. She had no idea, which, quite frankly, was a good thing.

"Amdusias was, is, a Duke of hell. Demon with a human body, with claw hands and claw feet, and a unicorn looking head. He's partly associated with sound and music and stuff like that. So it fits."

"So you think this is some sort of satanic thing going on?" Mel raised an eyebrow.

He shrugged slightly. "Not necessarily? At least not in the way you'd normally think. Could just be them trying to be edgy. Or I could just be deadass wrong." They both chuckled. "It just stood out to me, with all the discussions and delving into all the real life murders, and, and, and, disappearances, and, and" *stop stuttering* "world tragedies that the show uses in their story, that at least one of those fans would have brought it up. I mean, it wasn't that hard to find."

"Maybe it's some hidden thing that fans are supposed to find, but they are just too busy with all the other stuff."

"Maybe."

"It's like those things in movies. You know." Melody snapped her fingers and looked to her right, searching for the word. "Easter eggs! Can't believe I couldn't remember. You know. Like in the Pixar movies, where a character from one movie is like in a drawing on a cave in another movie. That kind of thing."

"Wait, wait, wait." He was excited. "I think, I think," he paused to stop the stutter. "I think you're onto something. The Disney thing. But not the Easter eggs. Umm." It escaped him for a moment. "Subliminal messages. Hidden things that you didn't necessarily register seeing with your eyes, but your mind knew they were there. Like the whole 'sex' thing in the dust cloud, or whatever it was, in *Lion King*. It's definitely there. At least on the VHS. I looked for it. Nevermind. That doesn't matter."

Melody was focused on him, her eyes wide at the speed and flow of his words. "Subliminal messages…" Melody refocused the conversation. She had her lips pressed tightly together in a smile to hold back her laughter.

"Right." He waved his hand. "This Amdusias demon was in charge of the 'cacophonous music of hell.' He could play music, but you wouldn't see the instruments. His voice heard in claps of thunder. That kind of thing. Kind of like hidden sound, right?"

"So maybe these people are using a podcast to experiment with subliminal messages?"

"It's possible. Makes sense. The only other thing I can think of, well, never mind." He dismissed his new thought with a wave of his hand. "Let's pursue this theory, and if it doesn't pan out, we can and deal with other ones."

Focus.

"So how do we find out if there *are* subliminal messages in the podcast?" Mel asked.

"I'm not totally sure. I know a little about sound editing and stuff, but nothing that detailed." He paused. "Hmm." *Owen maybe?* "You know? I have a friend that's a DJ. He does all that remix stuff, so he has all kinds of editing software. I don't know if finding hidden messages is even a thing he can do, especially without having the original multitrack, but it's worth a shot."

"We can't know any less than we do now, so, yeah! See if he can help!"

They chatted a little more before it was time for Melody to leave to pick up her sister. Before leaving, Melody gave his hand a brief squeeze. "Let me know as soon as you find out, okay? And… You don't have to wait until then to talk to me, you know? See you soon! Bye!"

"Bye." He was pretty sure he was grinning like an idiot.

He was still smiling later as he packed up his stuff and began walking to his car.

He started to unbutton his shirt. He shook his head and laughed at himself for "dressing up" like he had.

There. In the corner of his eye. He turned his head to the right to look. Someone was standing way down the road. He couldn't quite make them out, but he felt, no, he *knew*, this person was watching him.

He squinted in an attempt to make out who it was that was watching him.

Is that? Why would?

He set his jaw, and hesitatingly rocked back and forth. He took a halfhearted step towards the figure, who promptly turned and walked out of sight.

He bounced his foot and punched his hip once. He considered pursuing the figure, but turned back toward the direction of his car.

Pussy.

"Fuck you," he muttered, his smile now a frustrated frown. He wasn't quite sure if his words were directed at the watcher, or himself. Regardless, he turned his gaze to the ground and walked that much faster to his car.

***

The room was relatively sparse. A few anime wall scrolls, electric guitar, laptop, the desk it sat on, two chairs, and a bed. There was a faint smell of weed. Owen was giving the rundown on what he had managed to do with the podcast.

"So since I didn't have the original multitrack to work with, it kinda limited what I could do." Owen took a sip of beer. He lowered the can then scratched the back of his head with his other hand. His thick mane of blond hair was pulled up. At 6'4," he struck an imposing figure, but was more of a gentle giant. "Like you asked, I didn't listen to any of it, which also made it a bit tricky since, you know, it's sound editing."

"If anyone could do it, you could." He raised his can of beer in a gesture of a toast. He felt a little bad about possibly dragging Owen into a potential mess. Hopefully the beer worked as both a thank you and an apology.

"Yeah right." Owen laughed. "So here is the original file." He pointed to the screen. "I know you know what sound waves look like. Obviously the main consistent waves are primary dialogue. Other occasional patterns in between are probably background music. Big spikes are sound effects, or shouts, or something like that." They moved on to their second beer. "So, I did a phase cancellation, assuming the main talking was panned center. Which it was. Then I filtered out lows, highs, and mids. Basically did everything I could think of to remove any normal sound that would be there. I would have guessed it would've ended up as mostly just hissing noise, like during the empty spaces on a tape or vinyl, with the occasional subtle spikes from whatever I missed. But..." Owen opened a file named "final edit."

"That." He zoomed in on the track visual. "There is definitely something there still that I can't quite filter out. And it's constant with a pattern. No idea why. And it's present in the three other podcast files I checked. Makes no sense."

"Did you listen to it?"

"Hell no! First of all, you said not to, and B, you know I don't do that scary, spooky shit. That's your thing." Owen plugged in a set of headphones into the laptop and handed the headphones over. "Knock yourself out."

He put the headphones on and nodded to Owen to start playback on the file. The hiss of silence was there, as was the faint remnants of the elements that couldn't be completely filtered out. But he could hear it. Encased in the slimy, gelatin intestines of the remaining sounds, it was there. He felt a grimeyness creep up his spine and into the back of his neck. He pressed the headphones tighter to his ears and listened deeper. He couldn't quite comprehend or describe what he was hearing. All at once, like cicadas and drums and clicking of tongues and the resonance of a pipe organ. Rich and thick, it flowed through the hiss. At once bassy and rhythmic, yet cacophonous and irritating like too much ring modulation. These were not individual sounds overlayed: they were the sound. This was a voice. He was certain of it. There was a pattern, much like anyone speaking, but there were no discernable words. This voice was calling out. Repeating its message.

Listening to it felt like drowning.

He could feel the horrific cadence of the voice in his throat and chest. He felt a hollow feeling in his nose like he had just been punched there. The voice was constant and unrelenting. It crashed like waves into his ears, and pummeled his mind with intrusive thoughts.

Bash Owen's head in. Spill his brains out.

He pushed the horrific images and thoughts away, though he felt the guilt as if he had done those things.

He motioned to stop the playback, then handed the headphones back to Owen. He paused briefly, contemplating what he had just heard, before pounding back his beer. Immediately, he opened a third can, and looked at Owen, eyes wide, and shook his head in disbelief.

Owen transferred the files to a thumb drive, made sure nothing of those files remained on his laptop, then handed the drive over. "You alright, man?"

"I don't know," he replied, taking the USB drive. "I appreciate the help, dude."

"All good, man. Besides. Taking a little break from the sick Donkey Kong Country remixes I've been doing wasn't the worst thing."

They talked music for a while and finished off the beer. He thanked Owen again and went home.

***

He sat down on the sofa and took his phone out to text Melody about getting together to talk about the new discovery. They had been talking a bit more frequently lately, and he was thankful for that. He looked down at the open message on his phone, about to type, when he realized how tired he was. He wasn't sure what the mix of the beer, general insomnia, and the emotional drain of listening to that sound had done to his energy. Regardless, he didn't want to start a conversation during which he would more than likely fall asleep. He exited out of the texts, and set the timer on his phone for fifteen minutes. Making sure the countdown had started, he lay down, setting the phone facedown on his chest, and closed his eyes.

The ground was powdered clay. Dry and unstable. Browns and reds. The sky a deep crimson, seeming to shift from left to right, as if thin particles were being blown across the sky. Flashes of even deeper reds appeared behind the crimson canopy, like lightning hidden in a cloud. The air burned in his lungs. The stench of salt and sulphur stuck in his nostrils. The wind was hot and thick, but stung his flesh like ice water. He frantically scanned the area around him. A monstrous being lumbering on four legs. Taller than the jagged mountains behind it. Its flesh was colored in unholy greens and grays. Another being hovered in the sky. A twisting mass of impossible polyhedrons, pulsating and rotating around, and within, each other. Another creature with massive wings. Its face culminating in a knot of tentacles.

In the midst of these terrifying visions, there was another— closer than the others, but unseen. He felt this being watching him. Then he heard it. That terrible voice. No longer contained, the impossibly deep register of the voice assaulted his ears and body. Tingling and numbness spread through his arms and hands. The rhythmic pulsing struck his chest over and over, like he was standing in front of a speaker at the loudest of concerts. He gasped for air. He gripped his stomach. He felt like his stomach and intestines would drop out of him. The same sensation as if he were in a freefall. Stabbing pain pulsed within his inner ears. The cacophony of the being's speech tore into his mind. He felt what was like a thousand wasps inside his skull, attacking and stinging his brain. He became aware of every molecule of his body as he felt it start to pull apart. Though he could not see it, he could feel the presence of the being rush toward him.

He jolted awake as he raised his arms in defense. Several obscenities slipped past his lips. The sound of his phone hitting the floor helped snap him back to his full senses.

"What the hell?" He fell back, but didn't dare close his eyes again. He reached down for his phone and checked it. 3:45am. His arms tingled. He was drenched in sweat and shaking. He forced himself to move, to get up off the sofa. "It was just a nightmare," he admonished himself. He gritted his teeth and punched his chest once as he stumbled weakly to the bathroom. He was still shaking as he got into the shower. He felt sick. Deeper than the nausea that filled his stomach. He coughed and retched, but no vomit came. His nostrils still burned, and he could swear he smelled faint, dissipating wisps of salt and sulphur.

***

He was tired. He hadn't slept well in days. Although, that wasn't anything new, really. Sleep had a tendency to elude him. And, when he was able to capture it, it was usually fitful and riddled with bad dreams. This. This was worse. He was, though loathe to admit, afraid to fall asleep for worry that he would return to that place. He certainly did not want to hear that voice again, or feel that being watching him.

Melody had contacted him, wanting to meet up to discuss the latest discovery. He was somewhat reticent about it this time, however, mostly because he was worried about a possible argument over listening to the voice. There was no way in hell he was going to risk having what happened to him happen to her.

His head and shoulders drooped as he walked. He had taken migraine strength painkillers, but his headache persisted. His eyes felt heavy, and throbbed with discomfort and heat. He grimaced almost every time he took a breath. He rubbed his forehead with his hand and dragged it down his face. He shook his head, as if that would loosen exhaustion's grip.

"Hey! Wait up!"

A familiar voice. Hostile. His shoulders pulled up as his back muscles tightened. His left hand twitched, rapidly alternating between fist and open. He was already light headed, and could feel heat grow in his face. He hated confrontation in general, and this already felt horrible.

"You need to stop." Elliot approached him quickly and gestured with an aggressive point.

He was now sure it had been Elliot watching him that day after he met with Melody. It was Elliot that had become so hostile over the criticism of the podcast. They had had some unspoken falling out some months after, but he hadn't connected it to that incident until now. While he wasn't completely sure if that was the reason, he was certain he was about to find out.

"Stop what?" he asked with his own hostility and partially feigned ignorance. He had a guess, but regardless, he didn't want to deal with this shit right now.

"You know exactly what I'm talking about. You are always holding people back. Preventing growth in others. But you can't prevent this." Elliot smiled, his mouth and eyes just a little too wide. "Just because you weren't chosen, and refuse to grow, you try to stop others. But I am his prophet and shall lead them all to what we were and what we shall be again."

"What the hell are you on, dude?"

"You're pathetic," Elliot spat the words. "Too scared to move out from your little shell. Content in your routines. This is why you have no family. No friends." Elliot grinned. "You will always be alone." The vehemence of certainty and a curse.

He clenched his shaking fists at Elliot's words. He could feel the burning heat as he turned red. His vision became blurry, but he was sure he saw Elliot's eyes, just for a moment between blinks, change. In that fractional second, Elliot's irises pulled partially apart, like a cell in the midst of dividing, and the four new irises looked not unlike those of a frog. He started to back away, turned, and kept walking.

"We're warning you!" Elliot continued to shout. "You're nothing, and will always be nothing!"

Where did Elliot come from? How did he even know I was going to be here?

This was exactly the mess and danger he had been trying to avoid.

He made his way to the restrooms of the building. He couldn't stand the sight of himself. Face red. Tears staining his face. He gripped the counter and silently screamed. He wanted to put his fist through the mirror. He really wanted to put his fist through Elliot's teeth. *Why am I such a coward?* He hadn't stood up for himself. Didn't even seem to know how. He settled himself as best he could, splashed water on his face, and went to find a table outside to wait for Melody.

He sat at a table, one hand over his mouth, while he drummed the fingers of the other on the table. His foot bounced as he tried not to think about the events that had just occurred, yet obsessing about them just the same.

"Hey!" Melody greeted him with the same sweet smile as always.

He glanced up at her, then quickly looked away. He moved his hand from his mouth to the back of his head and rubbed. He shook his head and stretched his jaw.

Melody sat down next to him quickly. Her lips now in a frown. She grabbed his free hand. "What's wrong?"

He took a moment before replying. Partly to steady his thoughts. Partly to try and make sure his voice didn't crack or waver. He looked at Melody, his eyes wavered back and forth. He finally spoke. "Are you sure you want to continue all this? With me?"

"What do you mean?" Melody shook her head slightly.

"I mean." He tilted his head to one side, then the other. A habit he had when he was stressed. "I feel like I've dragged you into my world of crazy, and I don't really know where this is all leading. And I don't..." He swallowed hard and coughed once. "I don't want anything to happen to you because of me." His voice wavered and he felt a drop of water fall from his eye down his cheek. He turned his head away. *She thinks you're a loser.*

"Hey, hey." Melody squeezed his hand. "I don't know what happened, but I want you to remember something. I asked you to do all this research. So, technically, I pulled you into my crazy." They both laughed softly.

He turned his back to her and cracked a smirk.

Her eyes scanned his face. She smiled full and sweet. "I'm assuming you found something then?"

"Yeah." He breathed in deep. The heat in his face dissipated, and he no longer felt lightheaded. Melody had helped soothe him.

"What was it?"

"It's uh." He cleared his throat. "There is definitely a hidden message there. A voice really. Ancient. It's... calling out. Hearing it... messed me up. Had the worst nightmares after. It was beyond a nightmare, really."

"You aren't going to let me listen to it, are you?"

"Hell no." He dragged out the h sound and raised an eyebrow.

Melody smiled tightly holding back laughter. "It's good that you found something there though. Well, not good, it's scary actually, but, it kind of justifies something." She patted his hand and then retrieved a notebook from her bag. "I mean, we were just talking about crazy, and I kinda did something, well, crazy."

He scrunched his face and shook his head. He was genuinely confused at this point.

"Okay, so, I did a little research on my own." Melody gestured excitedly and opened up her notebook. "I found the podcast's offices, and the bookstore where the guy supposedly found the book that started it all." She turned the notebook toward him and tapped the page where she had written all the information.

He cocked his head while he read it. He heard her breathe out heavily, and he looked up at her.

"I bought us two tickets to Washington state." Melody grimaced as if expecting reprimand.

"You what now?" He turned his right ear slightly toward Melody, and leaned just a hint closer. He narrowed his eyes and turned them toward her.

"I know, I know." Cutely apologetic. "I probably should have asked, but I was excited, and I found cheap tickets. It'll only be three days. I arranged everything. Motel. Rental car. So, what do you think?" Melody waited for his answer. She scrunched her nose in expectation of a "no."

Sure, it went against his particular need for everything to be explicitly planned out in advance, but he had just had a vision of ancient entities of primordial evil— what was a spontaneous trip at this point?

"When do we leave?"

Melody smiled and clapped her hands.. "Yay!" Melody filled him in on the details. Relatively last minute, but enough time to make arrangements with work and everything else. With only one real full day there, there wasn't much they could really research, but they only had two solid leads anyway. He was determined to make the best of things, regardless of the dread that assailed him. And, despite the reason, getting away for a while, with Melody especially, was a bright light in the current sea of gloom.

***

They arrived without issue. All the usual processes of travel had gone relatively smoothly. They checked into their motel room. A single. Melody had chosen it because it looked less "suspicious" than getting a double or separate rooms.

She had been in the mindset, as had he, that they needed to keep a relatively low profile. They had given separate vague reasons to their respective jobs, kept away from posting anything about leaving on social media, and hadn't told anyone where they were going, much less that they were going somewhere together.

They settled into their room easily enough. They had packed light, and were keeping everything in their travel bags. No sense in unpacking with the limited time frame they had.

It was early afternoon as they drove to their first destination. Melody had found a business address for the podcast company. It was the only one apparently available, and it had seemed to be mentioned in their podcasts as their base of operations. It was easy enough to find with GPS, and public parking was fairly close by.

The building was strangely empty and quiet. They gave each other a confused look before finding the elevator and taking it to the fourth floor. They walked to the specified room number only to find a completely empty conference room.

Melody turned and opened her mouth to speak.

"Can I help you?" A woman's voice asked from behind, startling them, and breaking the silence and interrupting whatever Melody was about to say.

"Yeah. Umm." He turned to the voice. "We are looking for the office of the podcast group that works out of here. And, sorry, you are?" He could read her name tag, but still.

"Oh! I'm sorry! I'm Lucy." She extended her hand and shook both of theirs. "I'm the receptionist for the building. But, to answer your question, there aren't really any offices here. Basically this company offers small companies a business address, conference rooms if they need it, a place for mail to be delivered, and a real receptionist, that's me, to answer the phone. So, yeah, none of the businesses actually work here."

"Do you know the podcast people we are talking about?" Melody asked.

"I've seen their mail." She furrowed her brow and briefly looked to the left. "You know? I've never met any of them. Someone definitely picks up their mail, but it's never been when I've been here."

"Is that unusual?" Mel wondered.

"Not really." Lucy shrugged. "Just means they always pick up when I'm not here. Though I think I've met someone from every other company that uses us. Must be night owls or something."

"Do you listen to their podcasts?" He hoped her response would give insight into the truth of her statements. She seemed sincere, but he wasn't sure.

"Oh no." She shook her head. "I don't like podcasts at all. Too boring for me." Lucy laughed.

He nodded and exhaled through his mouth. "Thank you for your help, Lucy."

"Oh, you're welcome!" She smiled. "You two have a nice day!"

Once outside, Melody broke the silence.

"I'm sorry."

"For what?" He shook his head and leaned back.

"I should have researched more. I probably could have found out that the office building wasn't what I obviously thought it was." She waved her hand at the building. "And it's too late in the day to drive out to that bookstore now." She hung her head. "I feel like I wasted our day."

"Hey. It's no big deal." He leaned down and sideways to make eye contact with Melody. They smiled at each other and stood up straight. "Besides, we know for a fact now they are hiding behind another layer." He paused for a moment. "Look. It's not a wasted day if we just explore. Find cool things to check out around town. I mean, let's at least try the tourist thing."

Mel smiled. "You're right." She nodded. "I'm sure there are a lot of museums and coffee shops. And bars and restaurants."

"See?" He waved both his arms out, palms up.

"Ok! Let's do this."

They spent a little time looking up places to visit, and planned out the rest of their day.

The rest of the afternoon and evening were spent exploring the city. The "must see" sites. Markets. Coffee. Beer. Cuisine. They, quite simply, enjoyed the day, not mentioning the podcast or the surrounding issues. They talked about their interests and future plans, encouraging each other in mutual hope for the other's fulfillment.

They returned to the motel, and, after Melody, he showered, walked into the room, and tried to settle into one of the chairs.

"What are you doing?" Melody asked. She sat on one side of the bed and wrinkled her nose at him. She wore pajama pants and t-shirt, and had started to get settled herself.

"Uhh." His eyes looked around the room. "Going to try and get some sleep."

"In that chair?" She shook her head at him and raised an eyebrow. "Don't be ridiculous." Melody leaned over and patted the left side of the bed. "It's sweet that you are trying to be all... gentlemanly and all that, but c'mon."

"Okay, okay." He raised his hands in surrender. He swallowed hard and did his best to keep his hands from shaking. "Just hope you aren't a sheet-stealer." His voice cracked.

So stupid.

"No promises." Melody said with a light laugh and smile.

He lay down on the left side of the bed, and pulled his limbs tight against himself. He forced himself to stop chewing at the inside of cheeks and lips.

Melody switched off the remaining lamp. The only light in the room now was the flickering change of the television. Background noise from the low volume of the television and the air conditioning unit gently filled the air.

He put his right arm across his chest, and kept his left arm at his side. He almost gasped from holding his breath too long. His shoulders were pulled up off the bed.

She's just being polite. I should have just stayed in the chair. So stupid.

He felt movement. Melody took his right arm, lifted it up, lowered her head onto his chest, placed his hand on her hip, and then her right hand on his chest.

It felt unreal. In the midst of all this chaos, there was now, after so many years, a closeness he had been missing and longing for.

Don't overthink it. Just enjoy the moment for what it is.

"Goodnight." Melody said.

"Goodnight." He barely whispered and kissed Melody on the top of her head.

Mistake. Idiot.

He felt her smile and nestle in a little closer.

His shoulders finally touched the bed. He felt his own smile appear. And, for the first time in a very long time, he slept well.

***

The bookstore was several hours away. Thankfully, they had music, each other, and overwhelmingly beautiful scenery to occupy the time. Mountains, red cedars, and mountain hemlocks filled their view.

The town was small, quiet, and nestled in the woods.

He saw the store on their left, and pointed it out to Mel.

Mel pulled into the parking area in front of the store. The satisfying crunch of tires on gravel rose up to meet their ears. They parked in front of the store, under the "Used Books" sign, and got out of the car. With a little flourish of his hand and the slightest of bows, he opened the door to the store for Mel. She returned the bow, smirked, and stepped inside.

There were a few people perusing the store, which was fairly sizable, given how small the town was. No one looked up from what they were doing.

His nostrils flared and received the faint hints of vanilla and sweet, musky grass that wafted from the books and mixed with the cedar of the shelves that contained them. The bookcases were chest high, each with a double sided sign placed on top announcing what genre was stored there.

A mosaic of wood paneling covered the walls. Thin, light gray carpet covered the floor.

A pleasant mix of natural light and Edison-style string lights filled the store. Faint music floated through the air from hidden speakers. Presumably the musical stylings of some local artist trying to break into the indie acoustic folk rock scene.

They looked around the store a bit. At one side of the store sat the silvery cylinder of a coffee maker. A little sign that read "by donation" stood next to the packets of sweetener and creamers. He and Mel shared a grimace at the smell of the burnt, over-brewed coffee that emanated from the maker.

"Want some?" He raised his eyebrows twice in quick succession.

"Stop," Mel whispered intently and tapped his forearm.

There was a pop of static discharge, and he jerked his arm away. "Ow! Shit!" He exclaimed through his teeth, but kept his voice down. He grabbed his forearm, turned his shoulder towards Mel and leaned away from her.

Mel's eyes widened, comically frowned in surprise, and stifled a laugh.

They looked around quickly to see if they had disturbed anyone. Everyone appeared too engrossed in their own perusals to have noticed.

"Come on," Melody whispered. She smirked happily, still wanting to laugh, and indicated with her head that they should continue their search of the store.

His focus was soon on the "miscellaneous" section, with a slight hope of finding something interesting, or odd, for his own reading. Melody touched his back and let him know she was going to look around on her own. He nodded. They shared a smile, and Mel started walking to another area. His eyes slowly turned from Mel and back to the shelves. He grabbed and skimmed one of the more mildly interesting titles. He returned it to the shelf, and repeated the action. After the fourth attempt availed nothing of interest, he replaced the book to the shelf with a disappointed shrug, and then went to find the owner of the store.

"Can I help you?" A woman came out from somewhere in the back, carrying a few books.

"Umm, yeah. Do you run the store here?"

"I do." She smiled. She was probably in her late 50s and seemed pleasant enough.

"Okay. So. A while back, maybe eight months or so, a guy said he found and purchased an odd diary or journal here. Do you remember anything about him, or the book, or where it came from?"

"I remember that bright curious young man. Why do you ask?" Her smile persisted.

"Just a," he scratched the back of his head, "fan of his show. And I happen to also be interested in odd and curious things."

"Most of what you say is true, but I must correct you on something. He didn't find the book. It found him." She continued to smile at him.

"Umm. What?" A small frown and furrowed brow replaced his polite smile. He started to feel uneasy.

"And I know you aren't really a fan of his show." Her unbreaking smile started to feel wrong.

"How would you know that?"

"You aren't awakened." In between blinks her eyes took on the look of separating cells and were more frog-like than human. The same as he had seen in Elliot's.

"Oh shit," he mumbled as he slowly took a few steps back.

"You can't stop the change. Or his coming." Her smile had not changed, but now it appeared so insidious to him. She cocked her head. "He sees you."

It was then that he noticed the other patrons staring at him. Their eyes locked on him. Faces expressionless.

Melody, engrossed in some book, had not noticed.

He slowly, and deliberately, approached Melody, walking backwards toward her. Keeping his eyes on the now staring patrons, he placed his right hand on the small of Melody's back, and with his left hand, slowly lowered the book she was reading.

Melody looked at him, pulled her lips to one side and shook her head.

"We need to go," he whispered.

"What?"

"Mel," his voice still quiet, but stern, "we need to go."

Melody then turned her head to follow where he was looking. She didn't speak, but her eyes grew wide.

He gently turned Melody toward the door and they began to walk carefully. His right hand held her left while he continued to keep an eye on those that watched them. The owner still smiled from behind the counter. The patrons remained expressionless. Their heads turned slowly to follow their exit.

As he and Melody neared the door, the patrons' mouths opened, and that wicked ancient sound poured through. Of drums, and cicadas, and the clicking of tongues, and the deepest tones of pipe organs. He and Melody pushed that much quicker out the door and to their car. He had barely gotten in the passenger side and shut the door before Melody had the car started and put in reverse to back out of the parking spot. Gravel spewed out from under the tires. Melody hit the brakes and shifted into drive. A squeal emitted from the rubber against the asphalt. The bookstore and town soon disappeared from view.

The drive back took place in near-silence. The overcast skies were even gloomier now. The trees seemed to be twisting and curving toward them, like so many wicked arms. The mountains were all-imposing.

They barely ate that night. Their appetite and mood had been muddied from the day's experience. They made sure everything was packed and ready to go for the morning. They felt defeated. The leads had led to a dead end and a nightmarish threat. They lay in bed the same as the night before, but Melody clung to him for protection, not relaxation, and he held onto her in the same way.

He drifted in and out of sleep. The insomnia that so often assailed him returned.

He felt the presence before he saw it. Someone at the side of his bed. A low mutter, barely audible over the low volume of the television. The figure raised their arms up, and gripped something in their hands.

Pushing Melody out of the way, he threw his fist into the figure's stomach. The grunt revealed the intruder to be male. Melody stifled a scream as she saw him dive out of bed towards the figure, bringing his head up under the chin of the intruder. The axe, which Melody could make out in the flickering light of the television, fell to the ground. The scuffle continued briefly, and he knew it wouldn't be over until either he and Melody were dead, or the intruder was. He was able to find the axe, and, as the man rushed him once more, brought it, blade first, into the stomach of their assailant, cutting into his lower ribs. The axe went in much easier than he expected it to.

The intruder fell back, then collapsed.

"Melody! Turn on the lights. Mel!"

Melody snapped out of her state of shock.

After the brief moment of partial blindness, he could make out the intruder. A man in his late twenties, unfamiliar to both of them.

"Mel. Get our stuff and get the car started." He was shaking, but was surprised at how calm he was able to speak. He was light headed from the adrenaline and felt a little sick.

Melody acted quickly.

As Melody left the room, he moved closer to the body. *How did he get in? Could he have stolen, or been given, a key to our room? The security chain though... Does it matter really?*

He saw the intruder's eyes were the same as Elliot's and the bookstore owner's. Blood oozed out of the wounds, but it wasn't the deep red that would be expected. It was some sort of black, viscous liquid. And the smell. Like sewers filled with week old rotting meat, hot from the sun. He tasted bile in his mouth as he coughed. He wretched as he searched the body for clues. Wallet, keys, and nothing else. He took them and went outside, closing and locking the door. He spat out what remained of the vomit taste in his mouth.

Melody had the car started and was finishing pulling on a new shirt, smartly changing out of her pajamas. She jumped a little when he tapped on the passenger side window, but breathed a sigh of relief and unlocked the doors when she saw it was him. "You might want to change too." She smiled tightly, her eyes watery from the tears that formed there. Mel breathed shakily in through her nose and out through slightly pursed lips.

Hearing her words caused him to look down at his clothes. Some of the black blood had splattered on him. He changed as they drove. Once done, he looked through the wallet. A few cards and money, and *yes!* a driver's license. Oliver Samalson. The same first name as the podcast creator. This could be the key he was looking for.

Melody broke the silence. "Not to sound stupid, or ungrateful, but, I mean, why didn't that guy just shoot us? Why the axe?" Melody quickly wiped a few tears away.

"I think," he started to respond as he typed the address that was on the license into the gps, "a gun would have been too impersonal. Most of the murders that the podcast connects are all extremely brutal and violent. A gun for two people would've been too simple. And clean."

Mel pulled her lips to the side and nodded her head side to side. "That makes some sense."

"Whoever, or whatever, the murderers are making their sacrifice to, wants that personal, violent touch, I guess." He wasn't quite sure why the concept of "sacrifice" came out. Just what it felt like. "Drive here."

"Okay."

It wasn't long before they made their way into a neighborhood. Small, older houses, but in good condition. Wouldn't be a bad place to raise a family, he thought. "If it weren't for the psychos."

"What?"

"Nothing." He hadn't realized he had said that last thought out loud.

They finally arrived at the address on the license. Thankfully, one of the smallest houses on the street. Shouldn't take long to search. He found what looked closest to a house key on the keyring and, once they parked, they approached the door.

"What if there's a security system?" Melody asked right as the key slid into the lock.

"Then we run." He gave a wry smile and turned the key.

Click.

Turn.

Creak.

No beeping as the door opened.

He looked at Melody, tilted his head, widened his eyes, and sighed in relief.

They entered the house.

They made a quick search of the house. Living room, kitchen, dining area, bathroom, and bedroom in the back. No computer. No sound equipment. Nothing.

"Fuck. Fuck!" His anger got the best of him. After all of this, still nothing. No answers. He seethed as they stood in the bedroom.

"Hey. Hey." Melody's voice was calm and comforting. Never condescending or patronizing. She placed her hands on either side of his face and lowered his head so his forehead touched hers. "We haven't searched everything. Let's quickly check all the drawers in here, make another pass if we need to. There has to be something. Okay?"

"Okay." He nodded and exhaled evenly.

"Good." Melody smiled, leaned up, and kissed him on the lips. "You go left and I go right?" She pointed with her head to her left and to her right.

He couldn't help his chuckle and smile. "Yes ma'am."

Melody's thumbs lightly caressed his bearded cheeks before they turned to investigate their assigned directions.

"What do you make of this?"

A few moments had passed when Melody's voice drew his attention back. He came up behind her to get a closer look at the papers she was holding. Melody leaned back a little into him, her back against his chest, his left hand on her waist. Melody handed the papers to him and looked up at him with hopeful eyes.

"They look like purchase documents of a commercial property, maybe? Date is four months ago. Wait." He tossed the papers onto the desk and pulled out the keys he had taken. "Yeah. A Master Lock key and maybe one of these other two is a door key for the building at that address? We haven't found anything here that would take any of those. Feel like I'm reaching here, but maybe?"

"Could be why there aren't any computers, equipment, or books here? He moved them all there?"

Hope again. "Grab those papers and let's get out of here."

They locked the front door again on the way out, got into the car, and started driving. He plugged the new address into the GPS.

"So what are we going to do if this is the place?" Melody asked as she drove.

"Well. With any luck, we are gonna find the computer, remove the podcasts from online, and…" He paused for a moment. "Pull into that gas station. If we are going to put an end to this, then we need to make sure we are really going to end this."

They finally arrived at their destination. An older building. Two stories. Maybe a sub-level. He wasn't sure. There were several similar buildings in the area, relatively spread apart. The one in question was surrounded by a chain link fence. The gate was closed with a chain and lock. He got out of the car to, hopefully, unlock the padlock, as Melody switched the car's lights to only parking lights, so as not to blind him.

The key worked. He slid the chain free, and pushed the rolling gate wide enough for Melody to drive the car inside. He waved her forward, then pulled the gate closed again once she was through. He briefly debated whether or not to chain and lock the gate again, and decided on doing so. He got back in the car and they drove the rest of the distance up to the building.

They approached the door, armed with a can of gasoline and a box of matches each. He tried the first key. Not the right one. The second. A click and a sigh of relief. He pushed the door open and they carefully stepped inside. They were startled by the tink and hum of the automatic fluorescent lights which turned on as they entered. They looked at each other and laughed nervously. He turned to lock the door behind them, but where the other keyhole or latch should be, there was a solid metal disk.

The building was relatively large. A lot of ground to cover, especially with the urgency they felt.

There was a sub level, so they decided to start there, and work their way up. Once downstairs, they saw what seemed like a labyrinthine mass of hallways and doors, probably originally used to store whatever parts and supplies the factory had needed.

Of course he'd choose this place.

"We are going to have to split up."

"What? No way, Mel."

"How else are we going to get through all of this?" She gestured to the now daunting number of doors and hallways.

He wagged his jaw back and forth, looked away for a moment, and shook his head. It made him sick, but he knew she was correct. "Okay." He sighed. "But we need to be systematic. I'll take the left and you take the right?" He smirked.

Melody clicked her tongue and raised her eyebrows. "Of course." She winked, and smirked back.

They kissed, and Melody walked down the hallway. She turned right down a corridor, while he took the one on the left, which started several yards further up from where Melody had turned.

The first several rooms availed nothing. Old metal shelves with sparse remains of whatever had not been removed when the factory went out of commission. He only found the continued hum of the fluorescent lights, and the scent of stale air and rust.

"Come on, come on!"

He checked room after room. He grimaced and shook his head at each failure.

Then, finally, the second-to-last door on this side of the hall. Behind it was lamp light. Not the sterile fluorescent light that filled the rest of the building. Light from a monitor helped illuminate the room. The walls were covered in soundproofing material, including the inside of the door. The door slowly shut behind him. He barely noticed the hydraulic hiss of the door closer.

On one desk was a computer, professional microphone, and various pieces of editing equipment, from analog to digital. On another desk, books and manuscripts, many with strange symbols and imagery.

He swore he could smell the faintest hint of salt and sulphur mingling with the smell of electricity.

He set the gas can down on the ground as he sat in the chair in front of the computer. He canceled the automatic upload queue that was loaded with the next two podcasts. He found previous uploads on the server and deleted those as well.

"Are you sure?" the computer prompted.

"Damn right I am."

Click.

He stood, and as he did, noticed something to his left on the back wall. It looked to be much like a porthole window, sealed, and affixed to the wall. An out of place, circular break in the soundproofing.

There were strange engravings in the bronze colored metal frame of the porthole. The glass of the porthole itself had an odd prismatic quality to it.

He squared his jaw, approached, and looked into the window.

Behind the glass was an almost tangible darkness. Some impossible, infinite void where, if anything, another room should have been. Flashes of unearthly reds, like lightning within clouds, intermittently lit up the space.

He began to lose awareness of the room around him as he strained his eyes to look deep into the abyss. He gripped his stomach and steadied himself against the feelings of vertigo. He stared deeper into the darkness.

There. Much like in a dream, he perceived the being as simultaneously far away, yet close enough to touch. This beyond ancient creature, this being that up to now he had only sensed, came into view. It seemed to have no body as such. Just a mass of writhing and pulsating tendrils, twisting and undulating on and around themselves. Full of eyes and chattering mouths. Its grotesque, slick flesh appeared tar brown and puce in color as it reflected the flashes of light. The tendrils continued to twist and turn. Never stopping. Never resting. Growing. Feeding. Calling out.

He heard that sickening voice begin to fill his ears, overtaking what little sound was in this room. He could feel the being's desire for torment, violence, and despair. Intrusive thoughts tried to worm their way into his mind.

Worthless

                              Kill

    Die

                                        Destroy

He leaned forward, and braced himself against the wall with his left hand. He shut his eyes tight, fighting against the voice's onslaught. He roared over the din that was in his ears. He poured every drop of his own rage, pain, loss, and hate into his shout. His throat hurt. He opened his eyes and stared down the darkness in front of him. He slammed his right fist into the soundproofing next to the porthole window. He shook. Face red. A few hot, angry tears splashed on his cheeks. He looked into the being's eyes.

"It's over, you ancient piece of shit."

He grabbed the gas can, and began splashing gasoline on the back wall. The computer. The books and manuscripts. Pulling the chair with him as he made a trail of gasoline out the door. He propped the door open with the chair and continued to make a trail down the hall.

"Stop!"

Angry.

Hateful.

Elliot.

He turned to see Elliot holding Melody, arms twisted behind her, a serrated knife at her throat. He noticed small tears in Elliot's clothing and thin cuts with black blood.

Must have climbed the fence.

He stepped forward.

"No." Elliot tightened his grip on Melody's arms, and shook the knife a little, though not taking it far from Mel's throat. Elliot's frog-like eyes were hard and focused in hate.

He took his eyes off of Elliot to look at Mel, then looked back at Elliot. He put his hands up, and gave a nod. Without taking his eyes off Elliot, he slowly crouched down, placed the gas can on the ground and pushed it back. What gas was left sloshed around the container. He stood, and put his hands behind his back.

"I told you to stop this," Elliot continued. "I figured you, being the coward you are, would have given up. But I guess you found your confidence," Elliot sneered, "and your reason to push forward in *this*." Elliot jostled Melody roughly.

He stepped forward instinctively, but stopped himself when Elliot pulled the knife even closer against Melody's throat.

A small trickle of red blood ran down Melody's throat. Her nose twinged in pain, but she kept her jaw clenched in defiance. Her eyes remained open and focused ahead.

"Whatever you think you've done, you haven't stopped anything!" Spit flew from Elliot's mouth as he started to shout his words. "He and his brethren will return, and we who serve will be exalted and transformed!" Elliot grinned, and his frog-like eyes danced. "I gave you the chance to walk away, but you had to try and fuck it all up for everyone around you. You worthless fuck. Now you are going to lose the only important thing to you. I want you to see it. I want you to know, I want you to *feel* that you are the reason she dies."

Violent.

Brutal.

Personal.

He took his eyes off of Elliot and looked at Melody. Her eyes were as strong and as clear as the day he met her. They locked with his.

Melody smiled. "Finish what we started." Her voice was bright and unwavering.

He gave her the same wry, stupid smirk of a smile he always gave. His hands found the box of matches in his back pocket.

Hiss.

Flame.

Fire.

Heat.

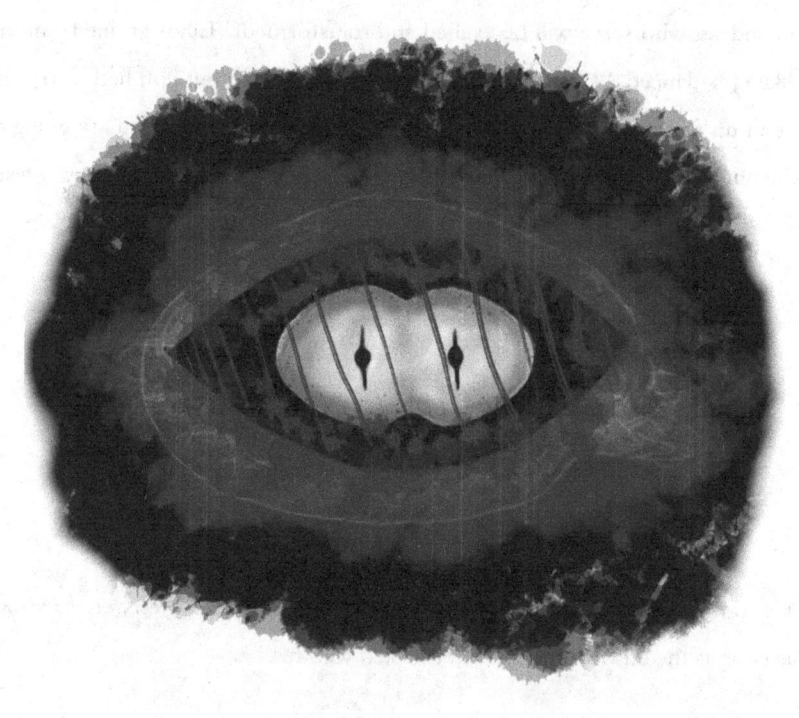

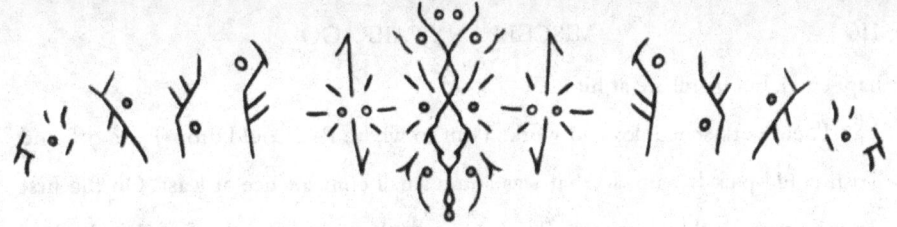

SUMMER CAMP

Paul and Trish argued in the bedroom. Not so much an argument actually, but it was more of an intense discussion than usual. They had always worked at talking through any issue that arose, and usually didn't fall into shouting matches, or the pettiness of cold shoulders. They had always said if a relationship was worth having, it was worth working through, or at least some variation of that.

Technically, this had all started three weeks ago when Tess, their daughter, had started summer camp. Paul had expressed general concerns about leaving their daughter with "strangers" for five weeks, which Trish understood. But, as Trish explained, several of Tessa's friends from school would be there. Plus, it wasn't like they had a lot of options. Getting a babysitter every day was going to be a logistical and financial nightmare, given the responsible sitters were all taking other, higher paying, summer jobs. A nanny was too expensive, as were daycares. The year leading to the current summer had been unforeseen disaster after unforeseen disaster. Paul and Trish were not big spenders, but their savings took a huge hit when they had to repair or replace their vehicles, replace the central cooling unit in their home, and the like. Trish had run the numbers and it was, as odd as it seemed, more cost-effective to pay for the summer camp than try to take time off work, or temporarily cut back on hours. Sure, they could possibly take from the small vacation fund they had put away to get away for four days before school started again, but, right or wrong, they didn't want to touch that money. They hadn't taken Tessa on a proper vacation ever, and wanted to finally do so, especially with her tenth birthday coming up.

Paul was stressed about the current situation. He felt like a bad husband and father, like he had failed his wife and daughter. Trish constantly, and lovingly, reminded him there wasn't anything he could have done to prevent all the things that had happened, but it still ate at him.

Their work schedules had worked out to where Paul could drop Tessa off, and Trish could pick her up, so that was some small convenience at least. On the first day of camp, Paul had brought Tessa in, went through the entire first day check in process, as Tessa waved to a small group of her friends that she knew from school.

The staff members were all female, headed up by Ms. Penytor, who was of an indeterminable age. Paul noted that she seemed simultaneously old and young. Otherwise, she was dressed unremarkably, save a few thin silver bracelets, and a necklace pendant of some dark stone.

Ms. Penytor greeted each parent and child as they arrived. Paul had a strange feeling from the handshake he received. It wasn't Paul's favorite custom to begin with, but her hand felt both hot and cold at the same time. Paul imagined, had the handshake gone on any longer, his hand would either wither and fall apart like a rotten log, or shatter, as if he had stuck it into liquid nitrogen. It was a brief moment, but it stuck in Paul's mind.

He said goodbye, reminding Tessa that "mom will pick you up, and I will see you tonight."

Tessa hugged her father goodbye. "Love you, dad."

Paul watched, with some trepidation, his daughter walk away to talk to her friends. Summer camp wasn't his, or Trish's first choice for Tessa's summer, but it was what it was.

As the next three weeks passed, Paul noticed Tessa had become more distant. She wasn't as talkative as she usually was, and mostly spent time in her room drawing. As amateur artists themselves, art and creativity were things Paul and Trish had encouraged in Tessa. However, Paul began to feel like it was more obsessive than a pure creative outlet, but he didn't know what to say, or do, about it.

On the Tuesday of the fourth week of camp, Paul was released from work early. He texted Trish that he was leaving work early and he'd pick Tessa up from camp.

Paul arrived about fifteen minutes before the official end time of camp. He went inside and stood in the lobby area.

The camp was held in a rented ballroom. It was large enough to have various centers set up around the room, in addition to a large main area in the middle for group activities. The children were all standing, facing Paul's left, and looked to be singing something. The wall and double doors separating the room from the lobby were all glass. The sound was muffled, but Paul could make out some of the words.

......moon burning bright

..........stars are right

....once what was.......

.................return....

A sing-songy cadence, not necessarily unusual for camp music, but this felt, the best way Paul could describe it, wrong. An involuntary shiver went up Paul's spine, and he suddenly felt cold. Granted, he couldn't hear everything that was being sung, but it certainly wasn't a song about being a good citizen, or taking care of nature, or having proper manners like Paul would have expected.

"What the fuck?" Paul quickly realized he had exclaimed out loud, and looked around to see if anyone had heard him. He was still alone in the lobby. He shook his head and looked back into the room. The children were done with the song and were milling about and interacting as normal. Other parents started to arrive to pick up their students as the children collected their things.

"Where's Mom?"

"Well it's nice to see you too.." Paul said, a little too sarcastically for his own taste. "Work ended early, so I came to get you so mom could have some time to do whatever."

"Okay." Tessa responded without any evident interest either way.

Paul, equal parts confused and hurt, followed his daughter out.

On the drive home, Tessa stared out the window.

"You feeling alright, Tessa?"

"Just tired, I guess." Tessa shrugged slightly, not breaking her stare.

"Alright. Well. If something's wrong, you know you can tell me or mom, right?"

Tessa nodded slowly, and Paul dropped it for the remainder of the drive home.

At dinner that night, the mood was down. Paul and Trish tried to have a normal conversation, while Tessa picked at her food. As she did so, she hummed the same sing-songy tune Paul had heard earlier. It was incessant and repetitive. It slowly grew a little louder as it went on.

Hmmm hmm hmm... Hmmm hmm hmm...

"Tessa. Please stop." Paul had not enjoyed hearing the tune before, and certainly did not want to hear it now.

"Tessa, hunny, can you eat something?" Trish asked calmly and kindly.

Hmmm hmm hmm... Hmmm hmm hmm...

"Tessa, your mom is talking to you." Paul's irritation had grown.

"Tess? Hunny?" Concern grew in Trish's voice.

Hmmm hmm hmm... Hmmm hmm hmm...

"Tessa!" Paul brought his hand down on the table a little harder and angrier than he had meant to.

The plates and silverware rattled and Trish whispered a harsh "Paul!" surprised at her husband's outburst.

Tessa snapped out of whatever hazey state she was in and looked at both her parents as if she'd just woken up. "Sorry, Dad." Tessa said and began eating.

"It's ok." Paul paused in partial embarrassment at his outburst. "And I'm sorry too."

The family finished dinner in silence.

***

"What's going on, Paul? You've never acted like that before."

Tessa was asleep in her bedroom, while Paul and Trish argued in theirs.

"I know. I know! It was that goddamn song, or chant, or whatever it is. It was the same weird song they were singing when I picked her up today."

Trish shook her head and shrugged not knowing what Paul was talking about.

"You haven't heard them singing some weird-ass song about the moon burning, and the stars, or whatever?"

"I've always gotten there after they've finished."

"Well, whatever. Regardless, Tessa's been acting a lot different the past few weeks. Sitting in her room drawing every moment she can. Walking around like she's in a, I dunno, hypnotic trance. Even you couldn't have missed that. "

"What's that supposed to mean?" Trish was indignant. "I'm a bad mother who doesn't know things about her daughter?"

"That's not even remotely close to what I said, or meant."

Trish raised her hand to pause the conversation and recenter her thoughts. "You're right. I'm sorry. I think, hmm, the stress of this year has gotten to me too. Look, hunny, we've always encouraged art and things like that, so her drawing all the time isn't the worst thing. And, yes, Tessa is acting a little different, I won't argue that, but she's growing up. Starting to be more independent from us."

"I would expect that at, like, sixteen, maybe thirteen, but ten?"

"Things aren't like how they were when we were growing up."

"Yeah, I guess." Exasperation filled Paul's voice. "You still have to admit the place is a little weird. That Ms. Penytor? Is she seventy or twenty something? It could honestly go either way."

"Are you attracted to her, or something?" Trish teased Paul.

"What? No!"

"Because I can't compete with g-milf status. Give me thirty or forty years, maybe."

"Oh my god, Trish. Stop." Paul laughed.

"I mean, if that's your new thing..." Trish pulled her lips into her mouth to emulate a woman missing her dentures. "Why don't you show me what you're working with, sonny?" Trish said in her best fake old lady voice, and tugged at Paul's belt buckle as he stepped back.

They fell onto the bed laughing, the tension of the night dissipated with their laughter.

Paul and Trish lay in bed, cuddling after making love, happy to have put their brief argument behind them.

"So, hey," Trish broke the silence. Her head on Paul's chest, as she lightly ran her fingertips across the same. "I'll talk to Margaret and see if she can work something out with my schedule for next week, so Tessa won't have to go back to camp. She'll probably have to finish out this week, but that'll be it. Then we will be on vacation after the following week, and the whole thing will be done."

"Yeah?"

"Yeah. We shouldn't have been so worried about the money. We will figure it out. We always do."

Paul felt relieved.

They kissed, turned off the bedside lamp, and fell asleep.

***

Paul's good mood continued when he received a text from Trish letting him know she had been able to work out the coming week's schedule with Margaret. An incredible sense of relief washed over him, and he felt a burden lifted. The whole thing may have been silly or blown out of proportion, but still, Paul was ecstatic that it was over. Work flew by that day, and Paul couldn't wait to get home to see his wife and daughter.

No one was home when he arrived, which wasn't unusual. Paul sent a text to Trish letting her know he was home before falling asleep on the couch. He woke up to a dark and silent house. Paul looked at his phone. 9:17pm and no messages. Paul rubbed the sleep from his eyes and got up. Maybe they had just let him sleep and went to bed early, Paul thought to himself. He turned on the hallway light and walked to his bedroom.

Empty.

Next, he checked Tessa's room.

Empty.

He hit the speed dial on his cellphone for his wife.

"Trish? Tessa?" Paul called as he searched through their home as the dial tone sounded urgently in his ear. His phone call eventually went to voicemail.

"Trish?! Tessa?!" His shouts grew louder and panicked. He dialed Trish again. Same result.

He walked outside the house. Trish's car wasn't there.

Paul called Margaret and a few others to see if they had spoken to Trish.

"Not since work," one said.

"I haven't, sorry. Is everything okay?" asked another.

"Just, just call me if you hear from her," Paul said.

Paul stood in Tessa's room, angry, scared, a horde of fears and thoughts stampeding over his mind and soul. He called the police as he looked at Tessa's drawings.

"I want to file a missing person report. My wife and daughter. They never came home tonight."

The drawings were of trees, seemingly the same drawing. No. Wait. They connected. Paul took the out of order drawings and began arranging them.

"Yeah, I talked to her this morning. She was supposed to pick our daughter up from summer camp, but I haven't heard from her since this morning."

A bigger picture formed.

"Yes, I've tried calling her. And I've called friends and coworkers. No one knows anything." He grew more frustrated.

Trees. Water tower.

Paul knew this place.

Stars. Red moon.

The middle page was missing. Paul quickly searched the desk, and found the missing page peeking out from under a book.

He put it in place. Paul's blood ran cold as he completed the puzzle. Small figures in a circle around some six-armed person, or thing, several times the height of the other figures.

"Tundle Field, behind the water tower. Please send someone. They're there. They are all there!"

Paul ended the call and ran to his car.

He drove as quickly as he dared. Paul did not want to risk getting pulled over before he arrived at the field.

The blood moon hung bright like a burning eye.

As Paul approached the field, he based his route on Tessa's drawing.. He kept the water tower on his right and eventually found other cars parked up against the fence that surrounded the field. He saw Trish's car, and quickly glanced inside the empty vehicle. He hopped the fence and ran as fast as he could toward the center of the field and the sparse trees that broke up the landscape. He had no plan, but Paul didn't care. His protective instincts drove him forward.

He began to make out figures in the distance. They became more clear as he approached. Parents he recognized from camp stood on the outer edges, perfectly still, as if under a spell. People in black hooded robes inside the loose circle of parents, free to move about, though they mostly watched the event unfold. In the center, the children stood in a circle, chanting the familiar tune.

It made Paul's ears ring and his head hurt, but he wasn't about to stop. He saw his daughter in the dim light.

"Tessa!"

One of the hooded figures turned to try to grab Paul, who instinctively punched the person in the face.

Paul continued to run past the high school volunteer as she collapsed, nearing the circle of children.

Paul slammed to a halt. He was lifted off the ground as some unseen force slammed its grip around his throat. Ms. Penytor approached— a symbol now glowing sickly red in the center of the black stone of her pendant necklace.

"So glad you could be here to witness the return. His time is long overdue. The barriers are cracking, and soon it will all be as it once was."

"Let my daughter go, you fucking bitch." Paul pushed through.

"Such language." Ms. Penytor let out a disapproving sound. "And in front of the children, no less!" She sneered mockingly. "Now see and behold and be honored to witness his return!"

Something formed in the center of the children—something dark and oily crouched down and hunched over. The air of the balmy night suddenly became frigid as the being manifested. Now fully formed, it unfolded upward until it reached its full fifteen feet in height. Its grotesque dark algae-like skin reflected the light of the blood moon. The creature stood on two, thin legs. Legs that looked too thin to support its matchstick body. Two small horns adorned its head, which was balanced on its long, thin neck. The only variance in its body was a subtle, ring-like protuberance that began several feet from its head, and tapered off evenly with its body.

Ms. Penytor chanted and howled in revelry, though Paul couldn't make out her exact words. His terrified focus was on the abomination standing before him. Ancient, unholy thing. A god returned to lay claim to what once was his. Its six arms suddenly reached up and out from its side as it let out a maddeningly triumphant sound.

Taking notice of Paul, the creature leaned toward him. Its movements were fluid, though unnatural. The ancient thing's featureless visage mere inches from Paul's horrified face. Its head moved as if it was sniffing him.

Paul could see his distorted, terrified reflection in the glistening flesh of the creature. The algae-like skin appeared to flow like some kind of black, fuzzy mercury.

Cloud after cloud of thick condensation appeared as Paul hyperventilated. A grimy and clammy cold coated and penetrated Paul's skin. His chest and lungs hurt from breathing in the freezing air. He grimaced at both the pain and the mildew odor that emitted from the creature.

The eldritch thing seemed to smile in delight at Paul's distress and fear. It laid one of its tridactyl hands on Paul's chest. The extreme cold of its touch burned Paul's flesh through his shirt. Paul could not control the scream of pain that tore through his lungs.

Satisfied, the ancient thing stood erect again, arms out, head back. It released another shout in some language that pushed Paul further into madness. A flash of darkness. Then nothing.

***

When the police arrived, they found a group of confused parents who had little-to-no memory of the day. The memories they did have were foggy. They had clustered together, trying to figure out why they were in a field with no recollection of how they got there. A few feet away, a woman knelt on the ground, holding her weeping husband, who, in between hysterical sobs, repeated, "It took them. It took them."

CELATUS DIABOLI

Eliza had to have it. As soon as she saw it, she knew it was the one. Pristine. Silken. Glistening like fine, soft strands of obsidian. It looked more beautiful than any piece of jewelry Eliza had ever seen— and this adornment, at least to her, was more valuable. It wasn't that Eliza was a particularly vain person. At first, in fact, she had been mostly uncomfortable with the idea of purchasing a wig.

She had dealt with grave's disease and hyperthyroidism her whole life, managing it, and never using it as an excuse for anything in her life. Eliza had always kept her condition to herself, when possible. She didn't want anyone feeling sorry for her, or treating her like some kind of invalid. In recent months, however, she had developed alopecia areata which had begun aggressively attacking her hair follicles, and it became difficult to hide such an obvious, and outward, effect.

Eliza's best friend suggested the wig.

"Eliza. Girl. It wouldn't hurt just to look," Bethany said. "I mean, you're going to be beautiful any way you decide to go. Bald. Headwraps. Hats. Wigs. I just think you should explore all your options."

So now Eliza was looking to purchase the most beautiful thing, wig or otherwise, she had ever seen.

Eliza had not intended to go shopping for a wig today. She had simply gone out to peruse various second hand shops and curio stores. There was barely any intent of necessarily purchasing anything at all. Sometimes something interesting would catch her eye and, if she could get a good deal, she would buy whatever trinket or clothing item that would cause some gleeful conversation and admiration from her and her friends.

In an almost dreamlike state, Eliza approached the register with her find. Eliza had a brief and quiet thought of confusion as to her current actions and state of mind. But whatever personal reflection was brewing was quickly squelched by the overwhelming need to purchase the wig.

"That'll be one hundred dollars."

"Oh. Yeah. Right." Eliza realized, in her eagerness, she hadn't even checked the price. She pulled her credit card out of her purse and handed it to the woman behind the counter. *100 isn't bad,* she thought. *Especially for a human hair wig.* Eliza wasn't sure why she had made that assumption. "Do you know anything about this wig?"

"I'm sure I don't, darlin'," the plump old woman replied as she swiped Eliza's card. She handed the card back to Eliza, and turned the point-of-sale device around so Eliza could sign the screen. The digital device seemed out of place, given the nature of the store. "Items come and go here. Some have stories, some do not. It's hard to keep track sometimes." She smiled as she handed a bag containing the box holding the carefully placed wig.

Eliza hadn't even noticed the woman deftly remove the wig from the mannequin head and package it up. There had been a brief moment she swore her signature on the screen had turned red, but she chalked it up to a trick of the light.

"Thank you!" Eliza raised her hand in a brief wave as she turned to leave.

"Of course, darlin'. Enjoy!"

Once she was home, Eliza prepared to try on the wig. With the excitement of a child on Christmas morning, Eliza could not wait to put the wig on. She placed a wig liner, made a few adjustments, then placed the wig, hair forward, on her head. She flipped her head back, sending the obsidian strands flowing down her back.

It was perfect.

Eliza, with no experience, somehow had the wig fitted and placed perfectly on her first attempt. And it looked...

Oh my god, Eliza thought, *I look good!*

Eliza had never been one to primp in front of the mirror, but she couldn't help but admire her reflection. Her default state of self consciousness quickly regained control, and Eliza felt a little silly. She hesitated, however, when she went to remove the wig. Eliza did not want to take it off, but, after a brief moment of struggle, she managed to remove it.

Eliza then realized she didn't have a mannequin head to properly store the wig, and was moderately annoyed with herself for not just asking to purchase the one it was on in the vintage store.

Eliza verified her uncertain recall that there was a costume shop not that far from her apartment. After calling to make sure they had one for sale, Eliza put on a ball cap and set out for the shop. She decided to walk because it wasn't that far and that was her personal favorite mode of transportation. She found her thoughts returning to the wig. Eliza wasn't sure how she felt about these minor, but borderline obsessive, thoughts about her new purchase, but she dismissed them as just being excited and nervous about a new endeavour.

Once she returned home, she carefully placed the wig on the mannequin head and smoothed out the hair. Even on the plastic blank face, it looked gorgeous. Eliza managed to pull herself away from doting on the wig to fix herself dinner, which she enjoyed with a glass of wine and her favorite show.

"So, I did it." Eliza had called Bethany to tell her about the day's big purchase. "I got a wig."

"You did? Must have been amazing. I know you and your picky ways." Bethany laughed.

"Shut up." Eliza laughed as well. "But yeah. It's like, I dunno. Perfect."

"You'll have to wear it Friday night then."

"Maybe." There was some hesitation in Eliza's voice.

"Eliza Constance," Bethany scolded, "don't you dare try and weasel out of going. We always go to Trouvere's, and this Friday is no exception."

"Alright, alright!" Eliza laughed. "I'll be there."

"You better!"

"Bye!" Eliza feigned annoyance.

"See you!"

Eliza's sleep that night was intermittent. She woke up several times throughout the night, with the vaguest hints of possible dreams. The only image Eliza could recall was something about a field. She was sure there was more, but it was dancing just beyond her memory, as dreams are wont to do. Eliza rolled over and snuck in whatever last few moments of sleep she could while the wigged mannequin head watched silently from the top of her vanity.

***

"Damn, Eliza! You look hot!" Bethany was always one to gas up her friends, but there was an extra dash of sincere surprise in her voice when she saw Eliza.

"Stop it!" Eliza responded with her standard self conscious, nervous laugh. Eliza wasn't wearing anything different than she normally wore when they went to Trouvere's, but even she, though she wouldn't have admitted it, felt more attractive than usual. Eliza was pretty, kept in shape, but never dressed with the intent of looking provocative or sexy. Cute, yes, but nothing beyond that. But she definitely felt sexier tonight. The only difference tonight was the wig. Eliza thought it might have just been a confidence boost from the perfection of the obsidian locks that cascaded over her neck and shoulders, but, regardless of the reason, she definitely felt more attractive.

"So what's the over/under on free drink offers tonight? I'm gonna put it at," Bethany looked Eliza up and down, "three and a half."

While drink offers weren't uncommon, Bethany's prediction seemed unusually high. They always got offers, though Bethany always got more than Eliza. Bethany was the hot friend, while Eliza was the "cute and sweet" friend. Plus, Eliza tended to turn down any drink offers, albeit with a polite "no, thank you," while Bethany tended to accept.

"It would be rude to refuse a gift," Bethany always said jokingly.

"You know, they usually aren't offering out of the goodness of their hearts, right?" Eliza would respond.

"Well, they shouldn't offer then. It's not a gift if you expect something in return."

"I'm sure they all understand that concept." Laughing sarcasm.

"Then they better learn."

Trouvere's was a jazz and blues club— the local hotspot for anyone that didn't really enjoy the dance club scene, or didn't want to go to the major bar chains. The quality of the music and the drinks were always high, and the atmosphere tended to be a lot more chill than other places. Though avoiding the hookup culture was virtually impossible, Trouvere's was better than most in being left alone when you turned someone down.

Eliza immediately felt eyes on her. She was definitely being checked out, by both men and women alike. Eliza somehow felt both uncomfortable and excited by the attention. She wasn't sure if it was always like this, or if she was just more aware of it tonight. Either way, she was here to enjoy her night with friends, and that's what she was going to do.

Eliza and Bethany met up with their small group of friends. They occupied a few of the small round tables that peppered the club. There wasn't a bad seat in the house— these just happened to be far enough back to enjoy the music, but still manage some level of conversation. Eliza and Bethany, drinks in hand, greeted their friends with the usual smiles, hellos, and hugs before sitting down. Their small group of now eight was an even mix of guys and gals, including Darren. Eliza had met Darren a few times before, as he was a friend of a friend of Bethany's. Eliza found him attractive, and found his quiet, though quick witted, ways intriguing. He seemed genuinely kind and shy, and their friends always had good things to say about him. Eliza and Darren greeted each other with smiles, a wave, and a "hey!"

Bethany, who had been encouraging Eliza to go after Darren, gave Eliza a little nudge and a wink, who responded with wide eyes as she mouthed "stop!" to her friend.

The drink offers started pretty quickly. Three men and one woman fulfilled the "over" on Bethany's prediction.

"Buy me a drink?"

"What?" Eliza laughed, half confused looking up at Darren, who had joined her at the bar.

"I just figured I'd mix it up." His own self consciousness started to show. "I, mmm, stupid dad joke. Sorry."

"No no no!" Eliza put her hand on his arm. "It was funny! I was just in my own world."

Darren smiled, a bit more at ease.

"Do you know this band?" Eliza gestured toward the stage.

"Yeah, actually. I mean, I'm about to sound like 'that guy,' but I saw them a few years back. The Light Hands. Really good psychedelic blues rock band out of Tennessee. Knowing a bunch of overly specific musical genres is kinda my thing." Darren coated the last statement in joking feigned pride.

Eliza laughed. "Well, good, because I know nothing about music. Well, other than if I like it or not."

They finally got their drinks and returned to the tables. Bethany, in full "wingman" mode, had moved seats so Eliza and Darren sat next to each other when they got back. They continued chatting, with Darren occasionally getting distracted by a song the band would play, which Eliza found endearing. They did manage to exchange numbers before a hug goodbye at the end of the night.

"So?" Bethany dragged out the questioning word. "Spill it."

"What?" Eliza laughed.

Bethany shrugged and gestured in a "seriously?" exasperated manner. Eliza failed to suppress her smile. "We are going to go to that Tuesday Night Food Truck Rally thing this week."

"Yes! Look at you, all confident and shit!"

"It's just a date."

"Mmmhmm"

"You are terrible!"

***

Once home, Eliza took off the wig, though she was reluctant to do so. She still felt it strange she was having such an attachment to a wig, of all things. Eliza figured the current fondness was exacerbated by the confidence it had seemed to give her. Regardless, she set the wig on the mannequin head, brushed out the locks, though it did not seem to need it, and then undressed and took a shower. Soon enough, she was in bed, relaxed from the shower, and sleepy from the late night and alcohol. Sleep came. And so did dreams.

A field. The same field as before. Bare feet on the grass. She could feel the moisture on the dark green and gray blades. A forest encompassed the outer reaches of the field. Their imposing, and mostly leafless, arms reaching toward the foreboding dark and cloudy dusk sky. A figure stood in the distance.

Eliza awoke. Her sharp intake of air and pounding heart startled her. She evened her breathing and settled herself down. Eliza was uncertain why the dream had frightened her so. The moon had perfectly placed itself in the sky to send light through the bedroom window, casting a silvery blue spotlight on the mannequin head. The light seemed to slowly cascade down the fibers of obsidian hair, like some etheriel waterfall. Eliza stared back into the blank eye divots of the mannequin head. Finally breaking her gaze, Eliza turned over to try to find sleep again. She could feel that it would now be elusive. Accepting defeat for that moment, Eliza decided to get out of bed, make herself a cup of tea, and finish the night on the couch with a show. Sleep eventually returned to her, their apparent quarrel over, and they spent the rest of the mercifully dreamless night together on the couch.

***

Tuesday Night Food Truck Rally was a success. Eliza found conversation with Darren easy and enjoyable. Even the silent moments were pleasant. The food was good too. The company was better. Though whatever local musician performed wasn't good at all. It was a fun and refreshing evening for both of them, despite the soundtrack of bad Tom Petty, Beatles, and Jeff Buckley covers. The night ended with a hug and kiss goodnight, and the promise to see each other again soon. Which they did.

They decided to go to the local farmer's market that weekend. The second date was as successful as the first, and soon time together became a regular occurrence. A day didn't pass without some form of conversation. They went to potluck and game night at Bethany's. Day trips out of town to distilleries. They went to coffee shops to just talk or be together while they read. They did dinner and movie nights at Eliza's. And there was, of course, Fridays at Trouvere's.

One particular evening, things moved past the usual cuddling during movie night, and Eliza and Darren made their way to her bedroom. Darren laughed at himself as he fumbled with removing Eliza's clothes. Between giddy laughs and reassuring kisses they soon undressed each other, despite their trembling hands.

They lay on the bed, and Eliza smiled and ran her fingers through Darren's hair as he explored her body. She felt him hesitate.

"Why'd you stop?" She looked down at him.

"It's just, uh," Darren breathed heavily, "I'm not used to having an audience." He nodded toward the wigged mannequin head.

"Don't be silly." Eliza chuckled.

"Hang on." Darren got out of the bed and took a few strides over to the vanity. "No offense," he said to the blank face and very gently picked up the mannequin head and turned in around.

Eliza jokingly rolled her eyes and shook her head at Darren as he hurried back to her.

Soon, the laughing and love making resumed while the wigged head watched their reflections in the vanity mirror.

A few months after their first date, Eliza and Darren made their relationship official. They spent more and more time together, and Elliza wore the wig more and more often.

It bothered Darren some that Eliza seemed to constantly wear the wig now, and he did try to broach the subject with Eliza. She had responded harshly, snapping at

Darren to not tell her "what to fucking do."

"Whoa, whoa!" Darren put his hands up. "I didn't mean it like that. Look, I love *you*, Eliza. You don't always have to hide what you are going through from me." He gestured to his own head. "I dunno. I'm probably saying this super shittily. Obviously."

Eliza, having returned to normal, was almost in tears, ashamed for having gone at Darren so harshly. "I'm sorry. I don't know what's wrong with me lately." Eliza had been uncharacteristically short tempered with pretty much everyone the past few weeks. She hadn't been able to quite peg what was wrong. She was happier than ever, but also angrier. She was unequivocally, and unexplainably, healthier than ever, but also, at times, felt sicker than she had ever been.

"Hey, hey." Darren put his arms around Eliza, who embraced him back. "Whatever's going on, we'll get through it."

They swayed gently back. Eliza looked up at Darren. "I don't deserve you."

"Now *that's* bullshit." Darren smirked.

They both smiled and laughed. They let out a mutual sigh as Eliza returned to resting her head against Darren's chest. She couldn't see the concern on Darren's face as they stood swaying in the embrace.

***

Another Friday, another night at Trouvere's. A new band played. The Latin and Island infused jazz blues swirled through the air. The male and female shared lead vocals, danced, and parried deftly, adding even more brightness and sensuality to the music.

Eliza had gone up to the bar. Looking back, she saw Bethany talking to Darren. He was leaning forward, hand on the back of Bethany's chair, eyes slightly squinted, gently nodding as he listened intently to whatever Bethany was saying.

Bitch. Eliza was shocked at the viciousness of the jealousy in her thought. She closed her eyes and shook her head briefly as if to toss the thoughts away. Eyes open again, she saw Bethany talking and laughing with the rest of their friends. Darren was walking to the restroom.

Eliza turned her attention back to the bar, resuming her wait for one of the two bartenders.

"Buy you a drink?"

Eliza looked at the man who had made the offer.

"I'm here with someone," Eliza responded. "Besides, even if I wasn't, do you think I'm going to owe you something because you bought me a drink?"

"Nope. Just like to buy beautiful women drinks." He then proceeded to order two gin and tonics. The man picked up one of the glasses, clinked it against the remaining one, before raising his briefly to Eliza and walking off.

Eliza stared down at the drink on the bar momentarily before a familiar voice broke her daze.

"Free drink?" Darren had returned from the restroom, and witnessed the tail end of the exchange as he had walked up.

"Something like that."

Darren pointed at the drink and shrugged a "why not?" when one of the bartenders approached for his order. Once completed, Darren switched out the drinks, giving Eliza the fresh one and taking the other. He sipped it, grimacing slightly at the taste of tonic water and juniper.

They drank in relative silence. Eliza eventually slipped her arm through Darren's, and laid her head against his shoulder as a slow, but heavy, blues song played.

"I need to talk to you, bitch." The slurred, angry words of an obviously drunk woman shattered the moment.

"Excuse me?" Eliza turned, shocked and confused.

"I wanna know why you were talking to my man."

Darren had started to move forward, but Eliza put her hand against his chest to stop him.

"Listen here. 'Your man' approached me, so why don't you go yell at him about why he's buying drinks for other women, or why he can't keep his dick in his pants.

Go bother someone else, you ignorant drunk." Eliza felt like she was observing from within, listening to someone else speak through her.

The woman stammered in anger, and stepped forward, intending to swing on Eliza.

"Os perdere." Eliza spoke, her voice simultaneously sounding like her own but also not.

As the woman made her first step, her ankle gave way as soon as it touched the floor. A snapping sound pierced through the music, followed by a nightmarish scream.

The woman was now on the floor, her tibia broken and piercing through her flesh.

Eliza, back to herself, was in horrified shock at what she was witnessing. Darren was in shock as well, though it was mixed with a kind of awe at Eliza defending herself, though her words might have gone too far.

The rest of the night was a blur. Eliza answered questions from the police as emergency services tended to the woman. All witnesses, including the security footage, confirmed the other woman had been the aggressor, and Eliza had not touched the woman in any way. The woman was heavily intoxicated, and the most simple explanation was that she had simply stepped wrong, lost her balance in the most unlucky way, resulting in the fracture.

Eliza nodded, barely taking in what the policewoman was telling her. Eliza was silent as Darren drove her home.

"Are you sure you don't want me to stay?"

"I just. I just need to be alone. Okay?"

"Okay." Darren nodded in reluctant understanding. "Call me, obviously, if you need anything."

"I will."

"I'll, uh, I'll call you in the morning."

Eliza nodded.

"Love you."

"Love you," Eliza mumbled as she slowly and robotically shut the door.

Darren lingered outside the door for a moment, uncertain of what to do. Frustrated at his inability to help, he turned away and went home.

***

A field. Bare feet on the grass. She could feel the moisture on the dark green and gray blades. A forest encompassed the outer reaches of the field, their imposing and mostly leafless arms reaching toward the foreboding dark and cloudy dusk sky.

A figure stood in the distance.

A woman. Naked, save a thin black robe that hung loosely and open over her shoulders. The decapitated head of a large goat covered her own, masking her face. Crimson ran down her neck and breasts. Long, obsidian black hair cascaded from under the goat head, and over the figure's shoulders.

Eliza continued to walk toward her, compelled to approach.

Eliza, now only a few feet from the woman, watched as she removed the goat head, revealing her beautiful, wicked, blood-soaked face. The woman discarded the goat head, stepping forward, letting the robe fall to the ground as she did. Her hand reached around the back of Eliza's head, pulling her forward, kissing her. Eliza tasted the iron of the blood on the woman's lips and tongue. Eliza tried to pull away, but she felt her skin had become fused to the woman's. She struggled in panic, but Eliza was pulled further into the woman, who had Eliza in full embrace. The two merged like some reverse mitosis, leaving the woman alone in the field, standing naked and smiling.

Eliza woke up hyperventilating. She looked around her room in a panic, her eyes finally resting on a moonlit, bare mannequin head. Eliza's hands went instinctively up to her own head and discovered the wig still on. Eliza figured, in the shock of the events of the night, she had forgotten to take it off before bed.

After turning on the bedroom light, Eliza sat down in front of the vanity to properly remove the wig. Bringing her hands up to the sides of her head, her fingertips ran through her hair instead of catching the edge of the wig to lift it off. Confused, Eliza tried again. The same results. She stood, the chair falling backwards, and leaned toward the vanity mirrors. Looking. Searching. There was no seam. No lip to lift. Only folicels and her own skin.

Afraid, and unsure, Eliza rushed to her bathroom. She grabbed a pair of scissors and began cutting away at the hair.

Snip. Snip. Snip! Snipsnipsnip!

Eliza attacked the fine strands furiously. She'd worry about making it look nice later. She just wanted to cut it back as far as she dared. Eliza didn't know how else to rid herself of it, and, in the moment, this was all she had. The deed complete, she set the scissors down, turned on the faucet, and leaned down to splash water on her face. The water felt good on her skin, and brought about the briefest moment of relief. She felt light, silken strands caressing her neck and shoulders. Shaking, Eliza looked up at the mirror and discovered her head still covered fully in long, perfect hair. The clippings that should have been on the floor were gone. Eliza collapsed in a corner of her bathroom and sobbed until she fell asleep.

***

Eliza stood outside the second hand shop, or rather, what used to be the second hand shop where she purchased the wig. She had ignored Darren's and Bethany's calls, as well as Darren's "Good morning, babe. How are you feeling?" and Bethany's "Checking in on you" texts.

Eliza had set out in the morning and was now in front of an empty storefront, with little evidence that anything had ever occupied the space. Eliza tried the front door, and looked inside, hand cupped around her eye and pressed against the glass as if searching would somehow bring the store to life, or prove she was mistaken in her observation that the store was closed and empty.

Her frustration gave way to resignation, which then gave way to an eerie peace. There were things she wanted, no, needed, to get, and she had all day to do it.

***

It was Sunday evening when Eliza finally returned Darren's phone calls.

"Hey! Babe! Been trying to reach you all weekend! Are you okay?" Darren was relieved to finally hear from her.

"I'm fine, my love. Why wouldn't I be?"

"I mean, it's been a, uh, unusual weekend."

"Let's go out tonight."

"Uh, yeah, sure! Where do you want to go?"

"Trouvere's."

"Really?" Darren couldn't mask his surprise.

"Pick me up in an hour."

"Yeah, right, sure." Darren paused. "Are you sure you're okay?"

"See you soon." Eliza hung up.

An hour later, Eliza greeted Darren with a deep kiss outside her apartment building. Her lips had a faint taste of herbs and honey, and Eliza was leading Darren to his car before he could fully process the thought.

Once at Trouvere's, they made their way directly to the bar. There were a few sideways glances from patrons, and a mildly surprised look from the bartender that had been there Friday night. Darren responded to a puzzled look the bartender gave him with an "I'm not sure either" shrug.

Eliza ordered two bourbons, neat, handed one to Darren, clinked her glass against his, and had her drink downed by the time Darren had finished his second sip. Eliza nodded her head in perfect time to the music and waited for Darren to finish his drink. As Darren neared his last sip, drinking a little faster than he normally would have, Eliza ordered two more. It seemed to Darren that the energy of Trouvere's was dulling, and only Eliza was in focus. The second drink done, Eliza's lips were on Darren's again. While the couple hadn't shied away from public displays of affection, this was much more than their usual hand holding or a light kiss on the top of the head. Eliza's fingertips lightly caressed the back of Darren's head, her honeyed lips and tongue intertwined with his.

"Let's get out of here."

Darren, while still confused at Eliza's current brazenness, was, in no uncertain terms, aroused. After leaving enough cash on the bar to pay for the drinks and a generous tip, Darren, led by the hand, followed Eliza out of Trouvere's.

It had begun to rain on their way back to Eliza's apartment, and their clothes were soaked, dripping water onto the floor of her living room. Darren had just enough time to take in the extraordinary amount of dried herbs and flowers hanging about the apartment. Before he could make a comment on Eliza's new choice of decor, her mouth was on his again, and her hands began to deftly remove his clothing.

Eliza had turned them around and began guiding them into the bedroom, still kissing and undressing. Now in the bedroom, Eliza pushed Darren's naked form onto the bed and finished removing her own clothes. The candlelight danced over Eliza's wet, naked body, and cascaded down her black hair.

The candles had been lit hours ago. The melting wax continued to drip down, building the warm stalagmites at the base of the candles. The slowly flowing wax seemed to move in time with the drops of water that trickled down Eliza's body. Eliza was on top of Darren, having put him inside her. She brought Darren's hands to her breasts. Her sexual aggressiveness was both disconcerting and tantalizing. The sounds of their pleasure mixed with the sound of the rain as it battered against the window. She moved Darren's hands down to her hips, as her hands slid up his stomach to his chest. Eliza's fingernails dug down into Darren's chest, piercing the skin.

"Damn! Shit!" Darren flinched and grimaced. He started to push himself up, but Eliza's left hand was now around his throat, pushing him back down.

Eliza's movements became more intense and forceful, as did her cries of ecstasy. She was leaning forward now, left hand on Darren's throat, and her right hand next to the pillow. The sexual energy rose to its peak, and, in the throws of mutual climax, Eliza brought the knife, which she had hidden under the pillow, across Darren's throat.

Darren's eyes were wide as he gasped his final gurgling breaths, blood spurting from the wound.

Eliza leaned back, back arched, and ran her now blood covered hand down her lips, neck, and breasts. The energy of sex, blood, and sacrifice filling her like a drug, as euphoric a feeling as the orgasm that had immediately preceded it.

Her body relaxed. She sighed in satisfaction and steadied herself with hands on Darren's lifeless chest.

Eliza opened her eyes and recoiled in horror. Her shaking hands covering her mouth, stifling a scream she was too shocked to release. She fell off the bed, crawling back toward it, sobbing. One hand covered her mouth as the other touched Darren's face, as if it would dispel the nightmare. That's what this had to be.

She retreated to the bathroom, attempting to wash the blood from her body. Her hands shook. She sobbed and retched. Not knowing what else to do in her dazed condition, she put on some clothes and headed to Bethany's place.

Bethany, after looking through the peephole to see who was banging so loudly at her door, let Eliza inside. The rain had washed away most of the remaining blood from Eliza's face and hands, but some remained. Her eyes sunken, skin pale, Eliza collapsed to her knees only a few steps inside Bethany's home.

"Eliza! What's wrong? Tell me." Bethany spoke kindly as she knelt next to Eliza, hand on her shoulder, the other rubbing her back, desperately trying to comfort her friend and to find out what was going on.

"Darren... I... I think I hurt him." Eliza started sobbing again.

"Eliza. Please. Talk to me. Where's Darren? What happened to him?"

"Why do you care? Are you fucking him?" Eliza's voice angry and jealous and not quite her own.

"What the fuck, Eliza."

"I'm.. I'm sorry..." Eliza broke down again. "I don't know what's going on, Beth. What's wrong with me?"

Bethany helped her friend up, and guided her to the couch. "Eliza... Look at me... Breathe, okay? In... Out... In... Out..." Eliza calmed enough for Bethany to feel comfortable stepping away for a moment to grab some towels, dry clothes, and her cellphone. "I'll be right back, okay? We are gonna figure this out, okay?"

Eliza nodded in response.

"Okay. Be right back."

Bethany went to her bedroom, grabbed a pair of pajama pants and a top, a few towels from the closet, and put her phone in the pocket of her own pajama pants.

"Okay. Let's get you dry, and..." Bethany's words trailed off as she saw Eliza standing in the kitchen with the large knife drawn from the knife block.

"Eliza? Sweetie? What are you doing?" Bethany's concern mingled with fear.

"I... I have to stop this."

"Eliza, please... put that down. We can talk about whatever is..."

"No! It won't help!" Eliza's shout was desperate. Too many thoughts. Too many images. She could feel and hear the hair moving and growing on her head. She rushed toward Bethany.

Bethany, instinctively shifting to her right, was knocked further out of the way as Eliza sprinted past her. Bethany heard the bathroom door slam shut and the click of the lock.

"Eliza! Eliza!" Bethany shouted and pounded her fist against the bathroom door. She slammed her shoulder into the door, which hurt her shoulder more than it made the door budge. Bethany kept banging on the door as she called 911.

The EMTs arrived first. One of them was able to kick in the bathroom door on the second attempt. They found Eliza curled up on the floor, the bloody knife laying near her. The EMTs, while they began to treat Eliza, found it strange that, despite the blood and gore of her now severed and exposed scalp, and the pain she had to have been in, had a look of relief on her blood and tear stained face.

***

"That'll be one hundred dollars," said the plump older woman from behind the counter.

"Gimme one sec…" said the young woman as she searched for her debit card in her purse. "…and here you go!" She smiled as she handed over her card.

The mannequin head on the counter watched silently, the long obsidian locks flowing like a waterfall of midnight.

OFF THE PATH

Albert decided it was too nice of a day to stay inside. Not that he needed much convincing to take one of his walks to the nature preserve that was near his home. It was just an extra beautiful day. It was most likely one of the last cool days of spring, so Albert figured he might as well enjoy it to the best of his ability.

He locked the door to his house and began walking. He welcomed the cool air as it hit him. It was a bit colder than usual for this time of year, but spring could be like that, and Albert certainly wasn't about to complain.

Albert walked, hands in the pockets of his zip-up hoodie, earphones in, cord trailing down to the phone in the front left pocket of his shorts. He enjoyed listening to music when he walked. It was calming to him. He liked to have a soundtrack to the cinematics nature provided: birds gliding across the cloud-streaked sky, lizards racing through patches of purple wildflowers, ants marching toward whatever food source had been discovered.

A wake of black vultures tore at the carcass of a possum on the other side of the road. A few of the horrific birds spread their wings wide, and hissed raspily at each other, fighting over who would get the next bit of flesh.

The breeze brought the fresh scent of death to Albert.

Albert grimaced and took a few steps to the right to widen the gap between him and the grisly scene. He hoped the vultures would be gone by the time he made his return journey home.

A few cars whizzed past Albert to his left, as he eventually approached the road leading to the preserve. The usual amount of people were out this morning, though Albert was a bit surprised there weren't more. He saw a few of the workers, he was never sure if he should call them rangers, moving in and out of the small visitor's center and talking to a small group of guests. Albert had never been inside the visitor's center. He had his routine, and he was fine with that.

Turning right, Albert followed the small path that led to the boardwalk that wound its way to the lake. Albert's normal route would take him down the boardwalk, where he spent a while observing the lake, then he would return home.

However, today the entrance to the boardwalk was blocked off.

Due to yesterday's storm, the boardwalk is closed. Sorry for the inconvenience!

- Staff

Albert hesitated somewhat awkwardly. While not completely unadaptable, he did like his routines. And when he had his mind set on something, he didn't particularly like deviating from the course. But, it was a beautiful day, and Albert didn't want to waste it by simply walking home.

His eyes drifted to a thick spider web constructed where one of the wooden posts joined the handrail. He stared for a moment in a kind of morbid fascination, though he did feel sorry for whatever hapless bug had gotten stuck and was now waiting to be a meal for a spider.

After his brief observation was done, Albert turned around and made his way back to the trailhead. Albert chewed at the inside of his lip as he tried to decide which direction to go. Two of the rangers, though still speaking to the group at the visitor's center, watched him. Albert, who had begun to feel a little stupid for not being able make a decision, wanted to avoid conversation. Thankfully, he suddenly felt an instinctive pull to the trail to his right. Albert hadn't gone down any of these before, so he figured he'd seize the opportunity to try something new.

He passed a few other hikers, and exchanged brief-but-friendly greetings. He passed an open shed on his right, full of a variety of rakes, shovels, and other gardening tools. Albert heard, then saw, a groundskeeper working up on the left, down a branching trail. Albert gave a quick nod in greeting when the groundskeeper looked up at him. Not wanting to walk in the heat of the sunlight, or to continue to interact with people, as little as it was, Albert drifted right, taking the trail that led into a heavy covering by the trees. In his peripheral, Albert was certain he saw the groundskeeper still watching him. The groundskeeper did appear to look back to his work as Albert neared the turn of the path. Albert soon saw a trail sign pointing to a sinkhole. His curiosity piqued, Albert made his way in that direction.

As he made his way further into the woods, his only companions were butterflies and the scattered songs of birds. The butterflies, some dressed in majestic orange, and others in glinting blues and blacks, seemed to dance to the music that lightly flowed from headphones in Albert's ears. He captured a picture or two with his phone, admired the beauty of the dancers a bit more, and then moved further down the trail. The scents of the woods danced on the breeze.

The coolness of the air along this deeply shaded path justified his choice of hoodie. It was relaxing, and made the walk more enjoyable. Albert looked up to watch the tree branches sway and bounce in the wind.

As Albert continued down the path, his shoulders pulled up as he felt the presence of someone approaching. Albert took two steps to the right and turned to let whoever was behind him pass.

The path was empty.

Confused, Albert took his headphones out and listened. He looked intently down the path behind him. Albert's back tightened and his neck bent to one side in a single, but intense, shiver. He scanned the trail and the trees again, but still saw nothing. His face scrunched in concern as a tingle pulsed from his chest, through his arms, and down to his hands. He felt goosebumps form on his arms. His nose twinged at the pungent smell of rotten eggs.

Albert told himself he was being silly and started to put his ear buds back in. He hesitated, shook his head, then finally put them back in his ears. He rubbed his arms to to rid himself of the lingering goosebumps as he turned back down the direction he had been headed.

The sinkhole had long been overgrown with vegetation. Trees and ferns jutted out, blocking any real view of the hole that was there. Not exactly what Albert was expecting, but not disappointing. He continued around, passing moss encased logs, until he reached the end of the trail.

He noticed, just barely peeking over the trees, the tips of roofs from the neighborhood that pressed so closely to the edge of the preserve. Albert wasn't against advancement, but he was grateful for the fortress of natural life keeping it somewhat at bay. After this brief reflection, Albert turned around and began walking back.

He continued past the sinkhole, now on his right, retracing his steps toward the entrance of the preserve. Some distance past the sinkhole, Albert realized he was walking in relative silence. The music was no longer playing from his headphones, and there was no longer any singing from birds. Confused, Albert removed his phone from his pocket.

Dead.

Albert was sure it was fully charged when he left his house that morning. He couldn't have been out here that long.

Albert shook his head in confusion. He placed the phone and headphones into his pocket, and he started walking again.

Albert felt impossibly tired. His legs and back ached. Albert wasn't going to be winning any marathons, but he wasn't in terrible shape. This sudden fatigue confused Albert more as he stopped to try and shake it off.

Glancing to his right, he saw a path that he hadn't noticed on his way to the sinkhole.

Was that there before? Albert thought to himself. Must have missed it.

Several yards ahead, the path narrowed tightly before quickly opening up to a small clearing. The path tapered off again at the other side of the clearing. A bench sat on the left of the path, facing ferns and clusters of trees. Albert found himself slowly ambling down the path toward the bench.

Even in his exhausted state, Albert could feel something was different. The trees still moved with the wind, but their rustling was agitated. Not the graceful sway like before. It seemed to have grown a bit darker and colder as well.

Albert sat down on the bench, finally relaxing. He found it surprisingly comfortable for a bench made of wood and stone. The wood was smooth and cool beneath his hands. He felt the pattern formed by the natural ridges and lines in the wood. He leaned back and looked up at the tops of the trees reaching towards the ever darkening sky.

The clouds above frantically raced and spread across the sky.

The agitation of the branches and leaves grew. A chorus of frightened, angry whispers from the trees cascaded down from all around and filled Albert's ears.

The hairs on Albert's neck and arms stood on end. The charge and chill in the air pierced his core.

Albert realized his jaw and neck hurt from the state of tension he was in. Any sense of his initial relaxation was gone. He wanted to go home now.

Albert pushed himself up off the bench to stand.

He didn't move.

A nervous laugh tried to escape his lips, but nothing came.

He felt he had become an extension of the bench. It was as if his body had intertwined with the wood he sat on.

Frantically, Albert tried to push, fall, or fling himself off the bench. He could feel the stress of his attempts, but he remained immobile.

He tried to call for help, but nothing but the faintest of frightened gurgling emitted from his throat.

If he could have turned his head and looked, Albert would have seen runes carved in the bench—faintly illuminated in a soft, sickly glow. And, had Albert studied such things, he would have realized that this bench, to which he was now bound through runic magic, was an ancient altar, given a new shape, but still used for its original insidious purpose.

Even if Albert could have looked, he wouldn't. His eyes were now transfixed on the horror that emerged before him.

From the thick of trees and ferns, an ancient creature pushed through. The gnarled and knotted hands gripped two trees as the head of the thing emerged. Its limbs twitched, and its head jerked, as it detected its prey.

Its head and face were made of four segments that joined together. Two branch-like horns extended from the top two segments, while the bottom two joined in an elongated point, giving it a goat-like shape. A diamond-like gap in the center of its face revealed a glimpse of disgusting flesh and thorny teeth. It had no eyes, but Albert felt its gaze.

The twisting branch flesh of its body was composed of gray bark, spotted with a flat curling brittle cinder like fungus. It lowered its over seven foot frame down to all fours. Its lengthy limbs jutted up and back like an insect. It approached him.

The sounds from the rustling trees was joined by the creaking from the limbs of the creature. The crunch of leaves and twigs beneath its feet. The chittering from it's horrid mouth.

The fetid smells of swamp, compost, and old dirt filled Albert's nostrils.

The segments of the creature's face opened up and back. A mass of teeth on the underside. The fleshy part did the same, and the creature began to devour the sacrifice left for it.

Albert could not scream— denied even that most simple of releases in the moment of his torturous death.

The altar and the creature accepted the offering. They were nourished and empowered by the blood, flesh, and gore that now splattered about.

From a distance, the groundskeeper and two of the park rangers watched as their new, but primordial, god fed. It was still weak, but through their worship, through their sacrifice, they would help restore the ancient being to its former glory.

The others will be pleased to learn of their progress.

Glory to Olcdaba.

www.ingramcontent.com/pod-product-compliance
Lightning Source LLC
Chambersburg PA
CBHW010640100726
47900CB00011B/2914